Mail Order Providence

Charlotte Dearing

The right of Charlotte Dearing to be identified as author of this Work has been asserted by her in accordance with sections 77 and 78 of the Copyright, Designs and Patents Act of 1988.

Copyright © 2023 by Charlotte Dearing.
All rights reserved.

No part of this book may be reproduced in any form or by any electronic or mechanical means, including information storage and retrieval systems, without written permission from the author, except for the use of brief quotations in a book review.

This is a clean, wholesome story of love and family set in late 19th century Texas.

Chapter One
A Concerned Cabinmate

Atlantic Seaboard, 1892

Caroline Shaw

Caroline Shaw walked the length of the SS Liberty. She strode briskly, or liked to think she did. With five days left in her voyage to Galveston, she was determined to strengthen her legs. The Boston doctors had promised that brisk sea air and daily walks would allow her to disguise her limp. She prayed they were right. For once.

The scent of salty sea air drifted on the breeze. Sunlight broke through the billowing clouds and dappled the sea. The boat rocked gently upon the waves.

Her companion, Beth, fussed and clucked about Caroline's husband-to-be. While Caroline pictured him to be a fine, upstanding, Texan cowboy, Beth had a different opinion of Nicholas McCord.

"Seems odd," Beth mused.

"What's odd?" Caroline asked. Why on earth had she breathed a word about her impending marriage? Her nosy cabinmate would not let the subject lie.

"I find it peculiar that Mr. McCord referred to himself as 'remarkably *handsome*.'"

"What's wrong with that?" Caroline bit her lip as she tried to picture her future husband. Part of her hoped he'd exaggerated. No one would ever call *her* remarkably beautiful or remarkably *anything* for that matter. Beth was a kindhearted girl, mostly, but since she'd learned of Caroline's Texas cowboy-husband she'd been overly inquisitive, like a great inspector. Too many questions! Beth was a better cabinmate than the other two women, at least. The Ashfield sisters went around with their noses wrinkled as if they'd just stepped in something unmentionable.

"It seems a tad vain." Beth gave her a pointed look as they approached the ship's bow. "Perhaps even boastful, if you ask me."

She wasn't asking, Caroline wanted to add. But then she realized with dismay she had done just that. It wouldn't have mattered. Beth was full of opinions, more so every day of their voyage to Texas, and she wasn't hesitant to share them with everyone.

Several sailors greeted them cheerily as they passed, tipping their jaunty caps. One made a show of bowing and offering a teasing grin. This happened often, especially when Caroline walked with Beth.

The sailors seemed to approve of the girls' daily constitutional. The first three days of the journey, they'd peered at them quizzically, but now they were all smiles, even the surly captain greeted them each day with a friendly word.

Caroline could hardly blame the men for their blatant admiration of Beth. Her glossy, chestnut hair was a straight as a pin and always tidy. Caroline's curls, on the other hand, had a mind of their own, especially after walking in the salty, humid sea air. Her brown tresses were never tidy. If anything, they defied any semblance of order whatsoever.

Beth took her arm. "It would have been nice if your mail-order husband had shared a little more about his looks. That way we could have been the judge."

"He didn't say much by way of specific details," Caroline admitted. "Simply that he's tall, over six foot, with light-colored eyes and sandy hair."

Caroline gazed across the sea. Usually the sight of the white-tipped waves soothed her worries, but with each passing day of the journey to Texas, she'd grown more fretful. She tried her best to think of Annie, the nine-year-old girl in Mr. McCord's care. Caroline's worries hardly compared to the plight of the young girl who'd lost so much of her family. First her parents, then her elderly aunt, who'd raised her up until last year when the aunt passed away. Her death left the small girl orphaned. Again.

"Humph," Beth muttered.

"What more do you want to know?" Caroline asked, trying to conceal her annoyance.

The last comment was meant to end the discussion. Instead, Beth saw it as an invitation to pester her with more questions about matters that were none of her concern.

"Is he a Christian?" she demanded.

"He is."

"Does he attend services?"

"Yes, of course. When he can. They live in a small town without regular services, but he attends whenever the traveling minister comes to Bethany Springs. He's raising his niece and feels strongly about setting an example."

Beth grumbled under her breath. The breeze skimmed across the indigo sea, carrying her grousing away. Thank goodness.

Beth meant well, perhaps, but her incessant questions and concerns troubled Caroline, to the point where she awoke each night, bathed in a cold sweat. She'd left her home in Boston to make a new life in Texas. In the beginning, she'd been swept away by the notion of healing her old injuries as well as caring for a motherless child. She'd have a home of her own as well as a family, something that had always seemed impossible.

Now, a few days away from landing in Texas, she was assailed by doubts, more every day it seemed. Caroline chastised herself. If only she'd kept silent about Mr. McCord, she and Beth might have enjoyed conversations that didn't constantly circle back to Caroline's impending marriage to a man she'd never met.

She tried to change the subject. "I finished the shawl I'm making for Annie."

"Who is Annie?"

Caroline drew a heavy sigh. She already explained who Annie was, time and again. But Beth was mostly concerned about Mr. McCord, not the little girl.

"Nick's niece."

Beth clasped her arm tighter and gave it an affectionate squeeze. "Oh, *really*? Is it Nick now? All along you've been referring to your husband-to-be as Mr. McCord."

"Oh, hush." Caroline laughed despite her embarrassment. "I still think of him as Mr. McCord. Mostly."

Beth went on. "So *very* formal. Tell me, are you going to shake his hand when you meet him in Galveston? Or will you give him a sweet, long-awaited kiss?"

Caroline tried her best to look indignant. "If you're going to tease me, I'm going to bed down in one of the lifeboats."

Beth set her hand over her heart. "And leave me with the Ashfield sisters? How could you be so cruel?"

Caroline arched a brow. "I mean it. No more teasing."

"All right, I'll stop."

Beth made a motion to show her lips were sealed shut. Which lasted less than an hour. After their walk, they returned to their cabin to prepare for lunch. Caroline searched her needlework bag to show Beth her finished shawl, a lovely, pale pink creation made of fine Scottish yarn.

The other occupants of the cabin, the Ashfield sisters, crossed the cramped chamber, eager to inspect Caroline's handiwork. The ship creaked as it cut through the choppy seas.

"I saved to buy this wool because I wanted to crochet something special for little Annie. Poor little lamb. She lost both parents before she could walk."

"It's beautiful!" Beth held it up to admire the delicate stitching.

Gladys Ashfield agreed. "It's lovely, my dear. Why, any little girl would be lucky to have such a shawl."

Bernice, her sister, chimed in. "I'm sure you two will be fast friends."

Caroline beamed at the women's rare praise. Secretly, she yearned to be more than fast friends with Annie. She prayed to be the mother Annie had never known, one day. Not immediately, of course, but eventually. Lord willing.

One of Mr. McCord's letters tumbled from her travel trunk.

"What's that?" Bernice asked, peering over her spectacles.

"Is it a letter from your Texas cowboy?" Beth asked as she reached down to retrieve the letter.

Bernice and Gladys chuckled and leaned closer, eager to know more about Caroline's husband-to-be.

"It's nothing of interest," Caroline said hastily. "Just a note, telling me about life in Texas."

"That sounds interesting to me," Beth said teasingly. "Is this one of the letters where Mr. McCord describes himself as handsome?"

Bernice and Gladys laughed and crowded closer, hoping to see for themselves. Caroline couldn't stand to hear them laugh about Mr. McCord or the subject of her impending marriage. It wasn't a joke. Not to her. To her, it was everything. All her hopes. All her dreams.

Without a word, she tucked her shawl into her needlework satchel and reached for the letter. She'd put it away and hope her cabinmates would leave well enough alone. But Beth wasn't ready to relinquish Mr. McCord's letter. Not yet. Instead, she turned slightly to keep it out of Caroline's reach.

The Ashfield sisters edged closer, both marveling at the fine handwriting.

"I'm sure he's a very nice young man," said Gladys. "What say you, Bernice?"

Her sister bobbed her head. "Very refined. Surprising for a cowboy if you ask me."

"I'm sure it's time for lunch," Caroline urged to no avail.

Beth's eyes widened as she studied the letter. "Your Nick has drawn hearts on his letter."

Caroline held her breath. She braced herself for Beth's laughter and ribbing comments, but her cabinmate didn't have her usual response.

"Seems peculiar," Beth murmured.

"What's peculiar now?" Caroline demanded.

Beth sighed and handed the letter back. "I've enjoyed my share of love letters, but I declare that's the first time I've seen a man adorn his letter with hearts and delicate, little swirls."

Caroline swallowed hard, uncertain what to say. In truth, she'd never exchanged letters with a gentleman. Who was she to say how they went about writing letters? She lifted her gaze to meet Beth's.

Instead of wearing a teasing grin, Beth regarded her with concern. Pity. Heavens how Caroline disliked it when people pitied her. She'd half-hoped that she'd left sympathy behind when she sailed out of Boston Harbor.

Beth took her hand and spoke quietly. "Caroline. Darling."

Caroline held her breath.

Beth spoke. "Where did these letters come from?"

"What do you mean? I don't understand."

"I suspect your husband-to-be, Nick McCord, did not write these letters."

Chapter Two
The Bounty Hunter's New Life

Nicholas McCord

Few things reminded Nick of God's glory more than quiet moments in nature. As a bounty hunter, he hadn't enjoyed nearly enough of these moments. Now, he relished the Lord's beauty more each day.

Especially when he spent time with his niece, Annie. The girl viewed everything with the wonder of childhood innocence. Well, almost everything. There was one subject that never failed to dismay the girl.

Standing a few paces from him on the edge of the riverbank, she sighed with disappointment. "I don't see why everyone thinks I need a mama."

Nick sat down on one of the knees of the massive Bald Cypress. The base of the tree was half on land and half in the river. The shade and breeze were a welcome relief to the warm fall afternoon.

"I keep telling you not to pay any mind to those ladies in town. They're a bunch of busybodies. That's all. Everyone keeps trying to lend a hand as if I don't know how to raise you properly. Check your line. I think you lost your bait again."

Annie lifted her rod. Sure enough, the worm was gone.

"I didn't feel a thing!"

"Pretty sure you lost it as soon as it hit the water. Want me to bait your hook?"

The girl shook her head. Quietly and studiously, she went about fixing a worm to her hook. This time she tossed it more gently. It settled in the darkest, deepest spot of the water, near the roots of the cypress. Almost immediately the line went tight. Annie yelped and yanked the fishing pole skyward, forgetting all the instruction Nick had given her about how to set the hook. The hook came flying out of the water, a small bass not much bigger than a minnow hanging and twisting in the dappled sunlight.

"Look at that," Nick marveled. "You win the prize for catching the first fish."

"But it won't be the biggest fish," Annie said. "Hopefully."

Nick reached for the line above the fish and drew it to him. "We'll see," he said. "Maybe we'll get lucky."

"Hope so. I could really eat some fish instead of eggs tonight."

"Well, this small fellow is going back into the river. He'll need to grow up a little."

Nick gently clasped the fish in one hand and eased the hook free. Fish in hand, he said, "You can look now."

Without looking, he knew that Annie would have her eyes squeezed shut. The girl loved fishing but was too tenderhearted to take a fish off the hook. He lowered down and laid the fish in the water, where it floated for a moment before it darted off.

The rest of the afternoon passed pleasantly enough but without so much as another strike. As the sun began its westward descent, they packed up and made their way back to the homestead.

Annie walked a few paces ahead of him, carrying the worm bucket as Nick followed behind. He scanned the Hill Country horizon and studied the wooded area that bordered the path. He was a vigilant man. Always. Ten years working as a bounty hunter had taught him some lessons he would never forget, and habits that would never die. Not that here, on his uncle's ranch, there was much need to remain cautious. While he'd made enemies during his years hunting down criminals, most of them had gone on to meet their maker or were behind bars.

As they neared home, Nick relaxed, and his thoughts drifted to the dream he had that morning. An odd dream that was as vivid as real life. In his dream, he saw a young woman, standing on a lonely beach, head bowed in prayer. She was in trouble. Of that, he was sure. When he awoke, his heart had pounded for a good while as he tried to convince himself it was just a dream.

By the time they reached the house, it was nearly dark. Without fish for dinner, Nick realized he'd need to patch together some semblance of a meal. If it were just a matter of feeding himself, that would be easy. Jerky and beans would be just fine. Annie had certain standards, however, thanks to his late Aunt Penny. The woman was a mighty fine cook, according to Annie, something she mentioned on more than one occasion.

"Maybe one of the neighbor ladies brought us a little something," Annie said, as if reading his mind.

"Sorta wish they'd stop being so helpful," Nick grumbled. While he wasn't a recluse, he was used to living by himself. He preferred to manage things on his own.

They climbed the trail up to the darkened house.

"If they did, they didn't light a fire to welcome us home." He tousled her hair playfully. "Guess you'd better make yourself useful while I fry up a mess of eggs."

Annie wrinkled her nose. He wasn't sure if the idea of a chore bothered her or the prospect of having eggs for dinner, again.

"See. If I were to marry one day, we'd come home to the smell of supper. I have a root cellar filled with food, but I'm not sure how to prepare half of it."

The girl said nothing as she trudged up the porch stairs. He noted the way her shoulders stiffened at the mention of marriage. He opened the front door and gestured for her to step inside.

"A momma would have a meal waiting for us when we get home."

"She'd never be a momma to me," Annie grumbled. "She'd always be a stepmother."

They went inside and paused in the dim entry to remove their boots. Nick might be a rough-hewn bachelor, used to moving from town to town in pursuit of outlaws, but he knew enough not to wear his dusty boots indoors and insisted Annie follow suit.

"What's wrong with a stepmother?" he drawled. Stopping by a nearby table, he lit the kerosene lamp. It flickered and sprang to life, making shadows dance across the parlor.

"What's wrong with a *stepmother*?" Annie asked with disbelief as if the answer were obvious.

He motioned for her to start on the fire. "Go on. You might as well work while you complain. That fire won't start itself."

Annie did as she was told. He left her to her task while he went about making something to eat. Eggs, bacon, and biscuits from the day before, hard as stones but softened somewhat by a moment in the cast-iron pan. Thirty minutes later they sat together at Uncle Theo's big dining table, taking up just a small corner. Nick said grace and they began their evening meal.

"If I had the sense to take a missus, we'd have fresh biscuits, not warmed-over biscuits." He winked and took a bite of bacon.

"In stories stepmothers are always bad. That's what Aunt Penny used to say. It was because they weren't related by blood. Not like you and me."

"Aunt Penny said that?"

Annie nodded, her big blue eyes sparkling in the lamplight. "She told me that after she read me the story about Hansel and Gretel." The girl started counting off other examples of wicked stepmothers, one by one on her small fingers. "She told me the same after she read me the story of Cinderella. Rapunzel. The Juniper Tree."

"Those are fairy tales, darlin'."

With that, Annie's lips curved into a sweet, innocent smile. "I believe in fairy tales, Uncle Nick."

Nick couldn't think of any response to her words. Silently, he watched her as she spread butter and jelly on her stale biscuit. She took a bite and murmured her deep appreciation, as if it were the most delectable biscuit she'd ever tasted, the little joker.

Moments like this made his heart do funny things in his chest. It was a mighty peculiar feeling. He hardly ever paid any notice to his heart. Bounty hunters need wits, instincts and quick hands. Hearts don't come into play when you're tracking down criminals. Up until a few weeks ago, he was a lawman, not a family man. Things had changed very quickly.

When Aunt Penny passed away, leaving him with a small girl to care for, he'd been more than a little surprised.

Resentful too if the truth be told. At least at first. She could have picked any of his McCord cousins there in Bethany Springs to raise the girl. Instead, she'd specified that he, Nicholas McCord, should be the one to raise Annie. Why him, he'd never understand. The Good Lord must have a plan.

Soon after he learned of Penny's last wishes, his cousin, Paul McCord, wrote him offering Uncle Theo's old homestead as a place to raise Annie. Apparently, Theo's final wishes involved the naming of a boy after himself, a new Theodore McCord, who would one day inherit Uncle Theo's favorite property, his ranch just outside Bethany Springs.

In the letter Paul explained that he and his two brothers had not named a child Theodore, and they had no intention of doing so. The house had been empty for over a year. Everyone agreed, the worst thing for any house was for it to be empty.

None of us like that the house is empty, Paul had said in his letter. *It would be a great favor to me and my brothers if you would bring Annie and turn the homestead into your new home.*

Nick accepted the offer with deep gratitude. With each passing day, Nick had settled into his new life. Things were turning out well enough, especially since few, if any, of his enemies knew he'd retired to the life of ranching in Bethany Springs. He preferred to keep it that way. Some of the men he'd collared were remorseless killers, men he hoped to never see again.

Nick believed in monsters, met several of them face to face, but he did not believe in fairy tales. Not like Annie.

Later that evening, he sat with Annie as she said her bedtime prayers. He bid her goodnight and made his way into the sitting room. The weather had changed, and a cool north wind howled outside. He relished the warmth of the fireplace as it chased away the early autumn chill. He wasn't accustomed to relaxing by an indoor fire but appreciated the comfort. At least he didn't need to contend with snakes, scorpions, and sundry varmints.

He did, however, have to contend with a sizeable stack of mail waiting for him on the rolltop desk. Sorting through the envelopes, he noted two bills, one from the mercantile, another from the feed store. Over the last few months, he hadn't charged much on the mercantile account, thanks to the generosity of friends and neighbors. Seemed everyone fretted that he and Annie would starve without a regular delivery of supper.

The bill from the feed store was a more considerable sum. Over the last few months, he and a hired hand had mended most of the fences. He'd purchased a few dozen head of cattle from a rancher near San Antonio and had ordered extra hay and feed to fatten them up for the winter cattle sale in Fort Worth. He intended to purchase more cattle soon. Come spring, he'd have a herd he could be proud of.

There was a letter which had been forwarded from a ranger out in El Paso, requesting his help with a pair of stagecoach robbers. Not too long ago, he'd have accepted an easy job like hunting down a few scruffy border bandits. Those days were over now. Someone would tell the El Paso ranger he'd retired soon enough, he figured.

At the bottom of the stack of mail he came across an envelope that took him aback. He got plenty of letters but couldn't recall the last time he'd received one addressed by a woman's hand. Probably not since Aunt Penny had written to him. Nick knew the letter was from a female the instant he spied it. The penmanship was delicate and feminine. What was more, it had a curious scent. Reminded him of cookies or Sunday afternoons when he was a boy. Or Christmas perhaps.

Like a fool, he sniffed it several times before turning it over to read the return address. Boston! Over the years, he'd met folks from all over, but he'd never met anyone from Boston.

He muttered under his breath, frowning with bewilderment.

"Who in tarnation is Caroline Shaw?"

Chapter Three
Nearly Gone with the Wind

Caroline

As they passed Florida and sailed into the Gulf of Mexico, the days grew warmer. The deep blue of the Atlantic Ocean turned to a light yet vibrant hue in the gulf waters. They made good progress. When Caroline encountered the captain, he often commented on the favorable winds and fine weather. She doubled her walks in hopes of continuing to gain strength. She liked to think that her gait was much improved. As much as she wanted to ask Beth her opinion, she refrained.

Out of pride perhaps, or fear that Beth would poke fun.

Beth, to her credit, was a steadfast companion as they took morning and evening walks. The sailors cheered the girls on. The captain would smile approvingly while scolding his men. He told them to keep their wits about them, despite the pretty ladies on board.

"Women on a boat," the captain liked to say, "can bring bad luck."

On the second to last day, just as they passed the port of New Orleans, Caroline and Beth very nearly brought about an unlucky incident. They were finishing their morning walk, heading back to their cabin when Beth loosened her bonnet. In that instant, a gust of wind tugged it from her head.

"I'll get it," Caroline said, trying to reach the bonnet before it tumbled down the deck.

She wasn't fast enough. The wind pulled the bonnet from her fingertips. One of the sailors dropped his bucket and charged down the length of the boat. Others joined in, yelling, shouting, and cursing at the mischievous sea breeze.

"That's my best bonnet!" Beth cried.

"Well, your best bonnet is about to join the fishes," said a nearby passenger.

Caroline hurried to the railing, just in time to see the bonnet fall over the edge. It did not, however, join the fishes. Instead of falling to the water, it caught on the length of the ship's rigging.

Beth came to her side and peered over the edge, murmuring with dismay.

"It didn't fall into the water," exclaimed one of the sailors. "It's not lost."

"Good thing too," said his companion.

The two men shared knowing looks. The younger one clambered over the side and lowered himself by way of a rope. A crowd gathered. Sailors shouted instructions and encouragement. The young man hung from the rope, some ten feet down from the deck of the ship and tried to reach the bonnet.

"Heavens." Caroline turned to Beth. "Tell them to let it be. No need to risk a man's life for a bonnet."

Beth pressed her lips together and knit her brow, unwilling to call the man back.

"Tell him! If he falls into the water, he'll break his neck. He's just a boy!"

"He's almost reached it," Beth argued.

To Caroline's horror, the young man walked himself away from the bonnet, then shimmied back, gaining speed before launching himself toward the bonnet, trying to swing close enough to grab it. The launch was clumsy, however, and the man spun fully around and slammed into the hull of the ship awkwardly. Everyone gasped, then breathed a sigh of relief as the young man looked up and said he was all right.

The sailors shouted and laughed, urging him to try harder. They offered cheerful insults as the young man struggled to reach the hat.

"I can hardly bear to watch," Caroline whispered.

"Almost there!" Beth called. "I'll give you a penny if you bring me back my bonnet."

The rest of the sailors cheered her offer of payment, egging on the young man clinging to the rope. Soon the entire throng of men were chanting the young man's name. Suddenly one of them produced a harmonica and began a rough tune. Meanwhile, the hapless boy struggled to reach the bonnet without losing his precarious hold on the rope.

"Hope poor Liam doesn't perish before he's ever kissed a girl," one of the sailors announced.

"Aye. That would be a shame."

The sailors all laughed heartily.

Caroline couldn't stand another moment of the spectacle. She leaned over the railing, cupped her hands to her mouth and called out a desperate plea. "Let it be. I'll give her money for a new bonnet."

The boy shook his head.

"Let it go, young man," she demanded, trying to sound more authoritative. "You're not strong enough."

For some reason, the men greeted her words with tremendous amusement. They roared with laughter. Even some of the male passengers joined in the merriment. The female onlookers, for their part, merely watched with curiosity, though Caroline wasn't sure if they were interested in the boy or the bonnet.

The young man scowled up at his fellow crewmen. He resented their laughter. At the same time, their laughter seemed to give him a renewed determination. With a final burst of energy, he kicked his legs and sailed far over the water churning below. Caroline's breath caught. He landed with a considerable thump directly beside the errant bonnet. He tore it free and held it aloft with a triumphant shout.

The crowd erupted with cheers. The men hauled the boy up and over the railing where he collapsed in an exhausted heap. Everyone turned to face Beth. They regarded her with expectation. Beth relished the attention and beamed with happiness. The onlookers parted to make way for her as she crossed the deck.

The boy offered the hat, holding it up as he lay sprawled on the deck. Beth tucked it under her arm and presented him with payment. She leaned over and spoke, presumably, a few words of thanks. The young man looked starstruck. He set his hands atop his heart and closed his eyes with a blissful smile.

The captain chuckled. He stood a few paces from Caroline. "Young Liam will never forget his first trip aboard the Liberty."

Caroline was shocked by the captain's response. For a careful and judicious man, he seemed unconcerned about the boy's risky antics. How could he treat his men with such little regard? Especially one of the younger sailors.

"He could have been hurt." Caroline shook her head. "That was entirely reckless. All for a silly bonnet."

The captain gave her a thoughtful look. "It wasn't just a bonnet, you see."

Beth returned with a triumphant smile curving her lips. "My thoughts exactly. It wasn't just a bonnet. It was my very *best* bonnet."

Caroline gave a huff of exasperation.

The captain spoke again. "I'm a Christian man, not prone to superstition, but many of my men fret about omens, bad luck and whatnot."

"What do you mean?" Caroline asked. She'd grown up in Boston but had rarely spent time near the harbor, so she knew few seafarers. She'd lived in an orphanage until she was old enough to work at the boarding house next door. Sailors were considered a rough and rude crowd, not suitable for a proper young lady's company.

The captain went on. "There are dozens of ways a ship can encounter bad luck. If any of the sailors are flat-footed, for example."

"That brings bad luck?" Beth asked worriedly. "Are any of *your* sailors flat-footed?"

"Of course not," Captain Wilson replied.

"I thought you said you weren't superstitious," Caroline remarked.

"Are you certain?" Beth demanded of the captain.

Both ignored Caroline as they discussed the matter.

The captain explained further. "I'm certain because I insist they prove it before I let them on my ship. I also never hire a sailor named Jonah. Or sail on a Thursday and definitely not on a Friday."

"What's wrong with Thursdays and Fridays?" Caroline asked, despite her indignation.

"Thursdays are named after the god of storms. And Christ was crucified on a Friday."

"What else causes bad luck?" Beth wanted to know.

"I don't let my men cut their hair on board the ship. Or their nails. No whistling into the wind as it beckons storms." He arched his brow. "And most importantly, given the near calamity today, never, ever let a fine hat blow overboard. Never. The magnitude of misfortune is governed by the value of the hat, and I'd venture things would have turned out quite badly had young Liam not retrieved it before it was lost forever. Good day, ladies."

With that, the captain nodded and took his leave.

For the rest of the day, Beth was quiet and pensive. They took their late afternoon walk with scarcely a word between them. She barely spoke during dinner. Caroline had to content herself with listening to the Ashfield sisters as they fussed and argued about each other's snoring.

After supper, Caroline and Beth went aboveboard to take their evening walk. It would be their last night on the ship. The next morning, they'd dock in Galveston. God-willing. Beth remained withdrawn as they began their walk. It was unusual for her. Perhaps she was sad about parting ways once they reached Texas.

Before she could ask, Beth took hold of her arm with a grip that startled Caroline. "I've been thinking," she said, her tone urgent. "My bonnet. It did blow overboard, didn't it?"

Caroline's thoughts spun with confusion. "Overboard?"

"It didn't fall to the water. But it went over the side of the ship."

"I'm sure it's fine. After all, you got it back."

"But only after it nearly dropped to the sea."

"I suppose it went overboard, yes, but Liam retrieved it quickly, so I don't think any bad spirits noticed," Caroline offered. She didn't believe a bit of what Captain Wilson had told them, but she could see how fearful Beth had become. She was pale. Her hands trembled. "It just went halfway," Caroline added, cheerfully.

"What if it brings about a calamity? Even half of a calamity?"

This was ridiculous. Caroline wanted to point out the absurdity of the subject but could see it would do no good. Instead of arguing, she began talking about Nick McCord, half-hoping Beth might return to her cheerful teasing. But even the subject of Mr. McCord didn't distract Beth from the certainty of impending disaster.

Later that night, after the Ashfield sisters had fallen asleep and snored in unison, Beth confided in Caroline. Sitting on the edge of Caroline's berth, she whispered, "I don't know why I'm so fretful about the silly bonnet. Perhaps my mind is playing tricks on me because I might be in the family way."

Caroline's breath caught. Beth was such an incessant flirt that at times it was easy to forget she was married.

"How lovely," Caroline murmured, taking Beth's hand.

Beth squeezed Caroline's hand.

"I've never imagined being a mother," Beth said quietly.

"Really?"

"Really. I've been married several months, to a kind and gentle man, but I've never imagined having one of Henry's children."

Caroline blinked, realizing it was the first time Beth had mentioned her husband's name.

"I love children," Caroline said quietly, hardly daring to say the words. "I'd love to hold a little one in my arms. It's all I've ever wanted."

Her heart crashed against her ribs. Part of her hated to say the words aloud. And yet she couldn't hold back. Children were her weak spot. Her undoing.

Beth sniffed. "It might be difficult carrying a child. What with your sore leg."

"True." Caroline drew a heavy sigh. "It might be."

Wasn't that what she'd heard ever since childhood? That she was weak and would not be able to do all the things other young ladies do, including motherhood. Beth had said it gently, but the doctors had been adamant – *you will never have children*. They had gone so far as to imply no respectable man would want a wife with an injured leg.

Back in Boston, she'd suffered with the cold and the damp. Each winter was harder than the one before. She'd made the journey south in hopes of strengthening her leg. More than anything, she prayed things would be different in Texas. Then again, Mr. McCord might simply want a mother for Annie and nothing more. In which case, it didn't matter if she walked with a limp or not.

"I can hardly wait to get off this blasted boat," Beth muttered. "It makes me queasy. Especially in the mornings. I can hardly bear it."

"It's just one more day," Caroline said. "And then we'll get off the Liberty."

"Hopefully."

"What do you mean?"

Beth shrugged. "My bonnet. It fell over the side of the ship. Not into the water, but close enough."

Caroline patted her hand. "Your mind is playing tricks on you. Superstitions are for sailors. Not reasonable, Christian mothers."

"I'm to be a mother." Beth grumbled as she got into her bed. "I hope I don't get fat. What if I get fat?"

"I'm sure you'll always be lovely."

"That's kind of you." Beth sighed. "I hope you're right."

Caroline smiled wistfully. For a moment, she dared imagine being a wife *and* a mother. Both seemed an impossible dream. Caroline would only allow herself to hope for one dream, not both. Heavens. That would be greedy. She'd marry Nick McCord so that she might serve as mother and caretaker for little Annie. Beyond that, she refused to hope.

No. Her trip to Texas was for Annie, not for herself.

She tried to imagine the girl. In her mind, Annie was sweet, demure, and gentle. She'd take one look at Caroline and from that moment on, they'd have an iron-clad bond, a love that could only exist between a loving mother and a doting, adoptive child. They'd join hands and spend a lifetime together, not linked by birth or blood but by the mystery of life's unexpected blessings.

Over the years, she'd heard every story about Texas, about the outlaws, and the cowboys and gunfights, as well as the rough menfolk and the riches they earned with the cattle trade. Texas was the land of opportunity. Ranchers made a fortune overnight. Streets were lined with gold.

She didn't care about the stories. She only cared about one story. That of Nick McCord and his niece. It might all amount to nothing. She might arrive in Galveston only to find no one had come for her. What then? She'd be right back to working in a boarding house.

Everyone in Boston had told her as much, from the ladies in the kitchen where she worked, to the caretakers in the orphanage where she'd been raised. Don't go, they warned. Texas is dangerous.

Her heart raced. Sweat beaded on her brow. As usual, her worries took off like the wind. Her leg ached despite all the walking. Her breath grew shallow and tight. Her concerns conspired. They caused all manner of havoc until she finally remembered one thing. One mighty solution. The power of quiet prayer.

In the dark of the cabin, she prayed for guidance. Not for her will, but for His.

With that, she let go of her concerns. The pain in her leg subsided. Her breath evened. She gazed out the porthole as her heartbeat slowed and her thoughts calmed.

The waves rolled across the sea, illuminated by the moonlight. The white crests stretched to the dark horizon. Stars dotted the night sky.

"So lovely," she whispered. "Only God could create such perfect beauty." Calm settled over her.

Too often she forgot to seek the Lord's comfort. Worries overtook her and brought doubt and pain. Only when she couldn't tolerate her own fear did she reach out to God. Why did she wait? God was always present, always ready to console her. She asked herself the same question over and over, never coming up with a satisfactory answer.

If only she could lean on the Lord *before* she was beset with fears. Not after. If only. One day, she resolved, she'd do better.

Before she closed her eyes for the night, she added one more prayer, for Beth and her unborn child. What a wonder. To think Beth had learned of such a miracle right there on board the Liberty.

Caroline smiled, trying to imagine the blessings that awaited Beth in the months to come. She snuggled under the covers. The boat rocked gently, the motion soothing as she drifted off to sleep. The peaceful night did not last, however. Sometime later, she awoke. The ship lurched and swayed more severely than they'd experienced since leaving Boston. Caroline lay in bed, hardly daring to move, wondering if she was having a bad dream. Time passed and the ship's turbulence grew more violent. Beth and the Ashfield sisters slumbered, blissfully unaware of the bad weather.

Over the next hour, Caroline dozed off and on. As dawn arrived, the skies remained dark as gunmetal. Her stomach knotted. She prayed and waited. The storm grew more violent. Thunder crashed. Out of instinct, Caroline changed her nightgown for a sturdy muslin dress, the same she'd worn since leaving Boston. Reluctantly, she woke her cabinmates. They rose from their beds, muttering with confusion. Caroline urged them to change out of their sleeping gowns into dresses and boots.

"Just in case," she said, trying to sound calm.

"Just in case of what?" Beth demanded.

"Just in case we need to leave the cabin."

The Ashfields sisters and Beth all grumbled. They wanted to return to the warmth of their beds, but Caroline wouldn't let them. She insisted they get dressed, using her most officious tone. It was unlike her, but she felt certain it was better to be safe than sorry, despite all the complaining.

Outside, thunder blasted, shaking the boat. Lightning lit the sky. Suddenly, the boat lurched. Shouts filled the hallways.

Captain Wilson's voice came from outside the cabin door. His tone was stern, urgent. "All hands. To the lifeboats."

Chapter Four
To Galveston for Answers

Nick

Nick awoke in an unfamiliar room. It took a moment to remember he was in a hotel room in Galveston. He and Annie had arrived the day before and taken a room in the Hotel Rebecca. He hadn't told anyone in Bethany Spring about traveling to Galveston. No, that would invite too many questions and he wasn't prepared to discuss the letter he'd gotten from Caroline Shaw.

Instead of asking others for information, he would put his bounty hunter skills to good use and get to the bottom of the mystery by himself. He always preferred to work alone.

As he lay in the predawn darkness, his thoughts wandered to the young lady who'd written the letter. He intended to send her away, but had to admit, he'd do well to take a wife one day. When he married, he'd do so on his terms. No way would he allow himself to get hoodwinked by some female he'd never laid eyes on.

His future wife would be meek and mild and as pretty as a picture. Not a woman who tried to trick a man into marriage with some mail-order scheme. No, his wife would be honest and, above all, devoted to Annie. That was more important to him than anything else. As far as he was concerned, finding a loving, kind-hearted wife would be as important to him as to Annie. Perhaps more so.

With the first rays of sunlight Nick woke Annie. They dressed and headed to the hotel's dining room. After breakfast, they drove the buckboard to the harbor.

"Galveston's pretty," Annie observed. "Lots of flowers."

"It's a fine town. Growing all the time. Pretty soon it'll be bigger than Houston."

His attention was drawn to her braids. It was clear he'd done a poor job earlier that morning. They were lopsided. One sat high atop one side of her head while the other perched low and behind her ear. The ribbons didn't match and were both frayed. Poor kid. She looked every inch an orphan despite his best efforts.

She gave him a sunshiny smile. "Why'd we come to Galveston?"

This was the fourth time she'd asked him. Persistent little child. She was a curious one. Though he couldn't really fault her for her inquisitiveness. After he'd read the letter, he'd lain awake most of the night and, first thing in the morning, prepared to travel to Galveston. He'd instructed Annie to pack a few things, find something to eat and be ready by nine in the morning. They'd set off from Bethany Springs in a hurry. She'd tried to hold her tongue, but it was a trial for the child.

"We came to Galveston on business." Nick kept his eyes fixed on the busy road, hoping to leave the subject at that.

Tucked in his shirt pocket was the letter he'd received from Caroline Shaw. Whoever she was. She'd written a single, bewildering letter that left him with a hundred unanswered questions. First of all, why was she coming all the way to Texas? She claimed she was a mail-order bride but that made no sense.

He'd never sent away for a bride and had no intention of doing so.

Caroline's letter made him a little hot under the collar, especially when she referred to, of all things, the letters he'd written to *her*. Where she'd gotten that notion, he'd dearly like to know. She sounded a tad young and innocent, judging from her wistful words. Either that, or she was a cheat and a liar like none he'd ever met.

Over the years, he'd had more than his fair share of dealings with the criminal element. He was more familiar with cheats and liars than any man needed to be. But in all his years, he'd only pursued cheats and liars that were men. He'd never tangled with the female variety. Till now.

Miss Shaw must not know who she was dealing with. He wasn't some wet-behind-the-ears, overeager, lonesome rancher. He was Nick McCord. Some called him a legend among lawmen. The idea made him smile with a swell of pride. Not that he liked to boast, but if others thought highly of him, he had to admit, it made him proud.

"Are we meeting someone?" Annie asked.

"Maybe. We'll see."

Nick didn't want to explain the matter of Caroline Shaw to anyone just yet. He'd look a perfect fool, talking about some woman who'd traveled to Texas to be his wife, some woman he'd never heard of.

At first, he figured one of the Bethany Springs busybodies had sent off for a wife. In his mind, there had to be a dozen or more suspects. Topping off the list was Aunt Sophie and her dear friend Amelia. But the list had more than two names.

Far more.

The woman who ran the mercantile insisted he court her widowed cousin in Boerne. The neighbor lady had a "darling" granddaughter in Austin. The rancher at the cattle auction claimed all sorts of handsome and agreeable sisters and cousins who would be pleased as punch to get hitched.

The way he figured things, the right lady would be hard to find. He wasn't even sure what he would look for in a wife, but after plenty of prayer, he was left with the simple notion he'd know when he met her. He had certain inclinations and instincts that were never wrong and had earned him a certain fame.

He turned the team onto the road that led to the harbor. The sea stretched along the horizon, blue and peaceful from afar. In the distance, ships of all sizes approached the harbor.

Annie pointed at the far-off ships with excitement. "Look at that, Uncle Nick!"

"Isn't that a pretty sight? We're about to see those ships up close as they sail into the Port of Galveston."

Caroline Shaw was on one of those ships, one named The Liberty. The ship, along with Miss Shaw, was due to arrive that very morning, according to her letter. It seemed hard to imagine, a young lady traveling all that way as a mail-order bride. She might be a hopeful bride, or she might be nothing better than a fraud.

Nick gritted his teeth, bracing himself for a meeting he couldn't begin to fathom.

Chapter Five
The Sinking of The Liberty

Caroline

After boarding the lifeboat, Caroline, Beth, and the Ashfield sisters found themselves being lowered inch by inch to the roiling waves below. Huddled together, they sat amidst other passengers of the Liberty. Early morning light had turned the sea to a dull, threatening gray.

With each crank of the pulley, the lifeboat jerked until finally the hull splashed down into the waves.

Instantly, they were tossed around violently. The rough seas served as a rude reminder that the storm wasn't done with them yet and might not be for some time. The strong wind persisted. Thankfully, the rain had stopped.

The icy, biting cold stole Caroline's breath. In an instant, she was chilled to the bone. As the lifeboat was rowed to the shore, she lifted her gaze to take in the site of the Liberty, which was clearly no longer sitting level on the water. It was lower on the front end compared to the back. People lined the railing, waiting for their turn to get off.

Vaguely, she considered the trunks she'd so carefully packed back in Boston. Everything she owned would soon vanish beneath the waves. She stared, transfixed. First off, there was Annie's shawl. Caroline had saved for months to buy the Irish wool. There was the stack of Nick's letters, adorned with hearts and scrolls. There were the modest dresses she'd sewn. There was more. A half-dozen or so books, painstakingly selected from sundry Boston booksellers, leatherbound volumes with guidance for the newly married bride.

All of it would soon slip into the churning water. All of it.

Her belongings were not the most important thing, she knew that, but she couldn't help feeling a powerful sense of loss. She closed her eyes and prayed to God, thanking Him for saving her and asking that all crew and passengers be saved, for she knew in her heart, the only thing that really mattered was that everyone survive, to one day hug, and be hugged by, their loved ones again.

The Ashfield sisters cried and held each other. Beth clung to her, digging her fingers into her arm. Caroline's teeth chattered. The lifeboat was slow going.

Thankfully, they didn't have far to travel. The Liberty had run aground on a rocky shoal that hugged the coastline. The land, be it Texas or Louisiana, Caroline did not know which, was hardly more than a few hundred yards away from the ship. The shore looked desolate and wild. She'd imagined this moment a hundred times before, stepping off the Liberty into her new life in Texas, but she'd never pictured arriving by lifeboat.

The trauma of the morning confused her sense of time. To Caroline, it seemed she'd heard the captain's warning just a moment before. And yet, it felt like days since she'd boarded the tiny lifeboat.

Finally, the lifeboat stalled on the sandy bottom, a dozen yards or so from the beach. The sailors tossed their oars aside, jumped over the side of the boat and into the shallow water.

They took hold of a rope that hung from the front, narrow prow of the lifeboat, slung it over their shoulders and pulled with all their might. Slowly, they dragged the boat and passengers to shore.

A fire burned on the beach. Someone had gathered driftwood and managed to set it alight despite the wind. The welcoming sight of a warming blaze made Caroline shiver.

One by one, the crewmen helped the women step off the lifeboat. Caroline marveled at their stoic, unwavering strength. She thanked each one. As soon as the last passenger was off, the sailors pushed the lifeboat back into the surf and began paddling back to the shipwrecked Liberty to rescue other passengers.

Cold and trembling, Caroline and the rest of the occupants of the lifeboat trudged up the beach to the nearby fire in hopes of warming themselves. No one spoke.

The wind gusted, blasting them with cold and flecks of sand. For brief moments the wind died, leaving them in an eerie quiet. Mostly, however, it gusted, leaving everyone with their heads down, hands holding on to anything that might blow away.

Everything, the strange wind, the desolate landscape, the ship sinking, all seemed like a strange dream. Caroline mostly fretted about Beth and her delicate condition. But the Ashfield sisters weren't doing well either. The elderly ladies struggled to walk in the soft sand.

Caroline kept hold of Beth's arm, doing what she could to support her but made sure to check on the ailing Ashfield sisters as they made their way up the beach.

Thankfully, the bedraggled group soon reached the fire, which was built near a sand dune that helped block some of the raging wind. Everyone rejoiced at the warmth. The Ashfields, along with Beth, found a spot to sit along the length of a fallen tree trunk. They rubbed their hands together, trying to regain some warmth.

As the afternoon wore on, the ship succumbed to the wind and the waves. Caroline and the rest of the passengers watched in silence as the ship slowly sank into the sea. It was a somber moment, but at least not one single soul was lost. Every passenger and crewman was present and accounted for.

All they could do was to wait for help to come.

After an anxious wait, wagons began to arrive. Passengers clamored for a spot, eager to reach Galveston, but the captain gave priority to the women and children. Somehow, he knew of Beth's condition and made certain she left on the first wagon.

Caroline saw her off, embracing her at the side of the rough wagon.

"Promise you'll write," Beth demanded.

"I promise," Caroline replied.

Beth didn't reply. Instead, she looked wistfully into Caroline's eyes as if for once words failed her. Caroline had to admit she too didn't quite know what to say. Silence stretched between them, along with the unspoken concern about Mr. McCord. Beth had suspected that he hadn't actually written the letters. Caroline decided she didn't care about that. All she wondered was if Nicholas McCord knew she was here, and if he would bother looking for her.

Neither spoke and a moment later, the wagon departed with Beth and several other young mothers. Caroline watched the wagon as it rattled down the road. It crested the distant hill, threaded its way between the scrub brush and disappeared.

Chapter Six
No Caroline Shaw, One Kitten

Nick

Maybe it was a case of nerves. Nick couldn't say for sure since he wasn't familiar with those sorts of troubles. On the contrary, he was known for his calm and steady disposition, but somehow, Annie, the little scamp, knew right away that he was fretting about something. She began pestering him with all sorts of questions. He hated the idea of lying to the young girl, or even of concealing important things from her, so he decided he might as well come clean.

"I received a letter from a young lady," he admitted. "A young lady who claims she's coming to Texas to marry me."

Annie stared. "You're fooling me, aren't you?"

"Would I make a joke about getting married?"

Annie didn't reply.

He shook his head. "Of course not. I'm telling you the truth. We've come to Galveston to talk to a lady who claims to be my mail-order wife. There you have it."

Annie's face reddened. She pressed her lips together and lapsed into a stony silence.

"Someone in Bethany Springs is playing matchmaker," he muttered.

"I hope the lady doesn't cry when you send her back."

Nick frowned. As much as he resented matchmakers trying for force him into a marriage, he didn't care for the notion of making a female cry. He had a strong disinclination towards upsetting ladies. He had to admit the situation was hardly her fault. Or was it? Maybe she was in on the scheme. Either way, he'd likely need to deal with a dust-up right there in Galveston harbor.

Dang it.

When they got to the harbor, he hitched the team, lifted Annie down and held her hand as they made their way through the crowd.

Annie walked with her arms crossed, her wrinkled forehead telling everyone that she was very unhappy. A moment later, her face brightened, and she smiled like she'd just caught the biggest fish in the river. She pointed to a crowd of children gathered round a crate.

"Look, Uncle Nick, someone's selling kittens!"

Lost in his thoughts, he looked around the busy harbor. "What now?"

"Kittens!"

He snorted. "Who sells kittens? And who would be a big enough fool to pay for a critter you can get for free."

"I wish I could have one," Annie said wistfully.

"You can go visit the kittens while I find out about the ship."

She agreed to his plan easily. Of course, it was never hard to persuade Annie about anything when it came to animals. He was grateful she obeyed him, especially with what lay in store. He didn't want Annie to meet Miss Shaw when she got off the boat. That was important, but he was also mindful of the rough, boisterous crowd waiting for the ship to arrive, a mix of cowboys, teamsters, and travelers.

He watched as she skipped over to the basket of kittens. Annie was a self-assured child, always happy to make new friends. Immediately, she began talking to some of the other children as they petted the kittens. The sound of their chatter and laughter floated across the crowd.

Nick turned to make his way to the edge of the pier. Of all the ships he could see, none fit the description of the Liberty. He scanned the area for the harbormaster or anyone who could tell him news of the ship. He listened to the various discussions and asked questions about its expected arrival. Nobody, it seemed, had heard anything about trouble or delays.

He waited, his impatience growing. He didn't like to be apart from Annie, but there was no helping matters. He kept a vigilant eye on the girl. She never strayed a single step from the box of kittens. The girl was riveted. He drew a sigh. It wouldn't be easy to pry her away from the box of kittens and he'd likely get an earful of how darling they were for days to come.

Finally, a shipyard worker arrived with news. The Liberty had run aground. The passengers were forced to disembark several miles up the coastline.

A murmur of shock and dismay moved through the crowd.

Even Nick felt a pang of concern even though he didn't know anything about Caroline. He'd only learned her name two days before and now he was waiting for her on a pier in Galveston. His thoughts turned with confusion. He wasn't entirely sure how to proceed.

The harbormaster went on. "We're sending wagons. Every passenger and crew member will be brought to Galveston safe and sound."

People clamored to know when their loved one would arrive.

"We'll get them here as soon as we can. Before nightfall I suspect. If you'd prefer, you can fetch your loved ones yourself," the man explained.

A murmur of consternation moved through the crowd. Many grew angry. Some of the women began weeping. Others stormed off, presumably to find the missing passengers rather than wait for them to arrive.

Amid the confusion, a gentleman shouted that he'd been robbed. With that, all heck broke loose. People began shoving and shouting. Demands for the pickpocket rang out.

Thankfully, Annie wasn't anywhere nearby. He ought to leave and let the bystanders find the pickpocket. His first duty was to keep Annie safe, not help find a thief.

Just then, a young man darted past. Out of pure instinct, Nick grabbed the boy by the collar. He stopped the boy in his tracks, practically lifting him off his feet. The boy choked and cussed a blue streak. He twisted and thrashed, trying to escape. In his panic, the boy dropped the man's wallet.

Another youngster appeared from the crowd. He'd come to defend the pickpocket, his partner in crime. Thieves often worked in pairs.

In the next instant, Nick was struck by a sharp pain on his arm.

With that, the pickpocket gave a final, desperate twist and slipped from Nick's grasp. Nick retrieved the wallet and returned it to the owner, brushing off an offer of reward. He didn't need a reward. He simply needed to get Annie away from this unpredictable crowd.

He hastened over to her as she admired the small kittens. Fortunately, she was so absorbed by the critters she'd missed all the ruckus.

"Ready to go, Little Bit?" he asked, trying to sound cheerful.

"Your girl seems mighty taken with the runt." A woman sat on a nearby chair, eyeing him with an appraising look.

"We're not interested, ma'am."

"Your little girl is interested. Mighty interested. That's my last one too. All the others been spoken for. Sure you don't want to buy it?"

"Not today. Let's be on our way, Annie."

Annie set down the kitten and brushed off her hands. She gave a small sigh and lifted her gaze to give him a sad look. She rarely fussed or talked back. And yet, Annie always managed to speak volumes with the tragic expression in her eyes.

"We're not getting a kitten, are we?" she asked.

"No. Not today."

"That's a shame," the woman told him. "A real shame. That's my last one and I need to get home. If I can't sell the kitten, I'll have to dispose of it."

"What does that mean?" Annie didn't know what it meant to "dispose" of something. She had no idea what the woman was suggesting.

The kitten rolled around on the grimy blanket, swatting at the loose threads.

The woman didn't reply. Instead, she gave Nick a meaningful look and tilted her head toward the water. Annie turned and looked at Nick, waiting for an explanation.

"You get my meaning?" the woman asked after a long moment.

"Yes, I do. I'd rather my girl not."

The woman shrugged.

With a heavy sigh, Nick dug a coin out of his pocket and gave it to the woman, narrowing his eyes as he paid her. "Guess we're getting a kitten after all."

The woman grinned. She glanced at his arm. "You're bleeding," she said.

Nick followed her gaze to discover a gash on his forearm. He knew he'd been stuck back on the pier but hadn't thought much of it. Now he saw the wound was deeper than he'd thought. Blood had soaked his torn shirt.

"I hadn't noticed," he muttered, mostly to himself.

The woman scoffed. "Be a shame if your wound festered."

He was pretty sure this nice lady was as slick a thief as the pickpocket. Seemed a tad peculiar to hear her talk about tending to some measly cut on his arm, giving him advice and whatnot. Right after cheating him out of a penny.

"I appreciate your concern," he growled.

"You take care now, Mr. McCord." He was startled at the mention of his name. It happened every time a stranger recognized him. He never expected it. What was more, he wasn't entirely sure if he liked getting recognized by strangers. While he was secretly proud of his fine reputation, he didn't care for folks knowing who he was.

She grinned, noting his dismay. "Everyone knows how you brought in Jack Masterson. Especially around these parts. He held up three stages between here and Houston."

"I don't talk about my work around my girl."

The woman shrugged. "He might soon meet his maker, if you get my meaning."

Nick nodded. There was little subtlety to the woman's choice of words.

"Come on, Annie," he said. "Take your new cat and let's get a move on."

Annie was so overjoyed, she hardly noticed anything else, not the topic of the criminal Nate had captured last year or the wound he'd gotten moments before. Annie was in her own little world. She cuddled the little kitten, holding it like a doll. Ever since they'd come to live at Theo's ranch, she conspired to turn the house, the front porch and the various barns and sheds into her own personal Noah's ark.

Well, it had to happen. Annie finally got a critter to love on. But one thing was certain, Nick vowed silently, he wouldn't get tricked into getting any more troublesome critters. The kitten was the first and the last. Of that he was certain.

All the way to the wagon, she talked to the little kitten, telling it how much fun they'd have when they returned to Bethany Springs. She promised to keep the kitten safe, letting it sleep in a basket right there in her room.

Meanwhile, Nick tried to picture the woman who'd written the letter. Was she safe? Frightened? There had been little news about what had actually happened to the ship and now he fretted about the woman he'd planned to meet.

That morning, he'd awoken determined to put an end to her scheme. Something had come over him just a short while before when he learned the ship was in trouble. His anger had softened. One option was to just wait for her to arrive with the rest of the stranded passengers, but he didn't care much for that one.

No, he and Annie would head east and find her, wherever she was. He'd explain the misunderstanding and how he wasn't interested in getting married. She'd understand. Of course, she would. And just as soon as he'd seen to her well-being, he'd bid her good luck and goodbye and head back to Bethany Springs.

With Annie. And the kitten.

Chapter Seven
A Prayer on the Beach

Caroline

As the morning passed, more wagons and men on horseback arrived. Thank goodness. At first it was just a trickle of people, a couple of buckboards, a pair of cowboys, a Texas ranger or two. The pace increased with each hour.

Caroline stayed close to the fire, both to keep warm and to comfort the other passengers as well as she could. As the wagons rumbled down the road and the drivers came to collect passengers, she studied the men with interest. At first it was because she hoped one of them might be Nick McCord, but after a time she simply wanted to compare them to the people she'd grown up with in Boston.

This was her first time seeing Texas menfolk and she had to admit she was curious, especially after every single person she knew in Boston warned her not to make the trip to Texas. Don't go, everyone said. Do not go to Texas. It was no place for a gently raised young lady.

They all told similar cautionary tales. The men were rough, uncouth, and altogether uncivilized. A delicate girl like her wouldn't fare well amongst the Texans. By delicate, she supposed they referred to her old injury.

She'd insisted they were wrong, of course. Texans might be a rugged lot, but Nick McCord was different. This, she had to believe. First, there was the simple fact that he'd taken in an orphaned girl. And next... well, she couldn't rightly say. He seemed decent. Kind. She'd staked her hopes on what she felt certain was true. That was, of course, long before she boarded the Liberty and met Beth, who'd proceeded to sow so many seeds of doubt.

Dismay wrapped tighter around Caroline's heart. She was alone. Many passengers remained stranded on the beach, but she knew almost none of them. A fair number were immigrants from Germany, Sweden and Scotland. They were decent folk but preferred to keep to themselves.

She turned away from the huddled groups of passengers and crew. Wandering toward the beach, she eyed the endless stretch of sea. The storm had rolled off to distant parts and had left a calm sea in its wake. Waves rolled to the shore, lapping across the smooth sand.

A gentle breeze washed over her. It was warmer than the winds they'd suffered earlier. It brought a sort of calm, much to Caroline's surprise. Closing her eyes, she prayed, asking God to give her strength.

Lord, you gave me the will and fortitude to set out on this journey. I depend on Your love and guidance. Please help me find my way. Please let me serve You as well as my new husband and child.

A sense of peace fell over her. Quiet filled her heart. She drew a deep breath, eyes closed, relishing the relief that only prayer could offer. The breeze washed over her, bringing with it a sense of peace she hadn't had since leaving home.

Chapter Eight
News of Caroline Shaw

Nick

The kitten was a mistake. He regretted buying it almost immediately, not that he'd say the harsh words aloud. Annie would never forgive him. Land sakes. The girl had been chattering about the kitten non-stop. Even as they left the harbor, she'd carried on.

At first it had seemed harmless. He'd been too distracted to pay much attention, but he recalled vaguely that the kitten was sweet and maybe even charming. That was back at the pier. Somewhere along the way it had turned into a tiny, furry devil.

The trouble started when Nick flicked the reins, and the team pulled against the harness. All well and good, but the jerk of the wagon spooked the kitten. It leapt out of Annie's arms and climbed up his back, its tiny claws stabbing him with every step. It mewed piteously but then found a spot on his shoulder and nestled against his neck.

"He really likes you," Annie remarked.

Nick growled softly.

"He really seems fond of you." Annie laughed with delight.

"Just what I wanted. A kitten that's fond of me."

"He's purring. I can hear it even with all the other noise."

Wagons and riders filled the streets. People were coming and going in a steady stream. They shouted and called to each other in German, Spanish and what he figured might be Polish or Czech. Galveston received tens of thousands of immigrants every year.

None of them seemed to know how to drive a wagon, he decided as he swerved to miss a parked buckboard. The kitten tensed and dug needle-point claws into his shoulder. He drew a sharp breath.

"Why don't you take your kitten, Little Bit?" he suggested.

"He looks so happy up on your shoulder."

Nick grumbled under his breath. The kitten was a nuisance. So was the mail-order bride he was setting out to talk to, but there it was. The day was a day for trouble and there was no helping matters.

"Slow down, Uncle Nick. Kittens don't like to go fast."

Nick ignored her suggestion. He didn't want to slow down. He was in a hurry for some reason. Once he'd seen Miss Shaw for himself and made certain she was safe, he'd arrange for her to stay in Galveston or return to Boston. Whatever she decided. He didn't care one way or another.

The kitten settled on his shoulder and seemed to slip into an afternoon nap. Or so he hoped. At least, it had stopped stabbing him with its vicious claws. Annie kept smiling at him, happy as a lamb in clover. The girl's happiness made it all worthwhile.

After they left the town of Galveston, they turned eastward, taking a road that would lead to Houston. It was well-traveled, but it was hard to say how many folks headed to Houston and how many went to retrieve the ship-wrecked passengers of the Liberty.

Along the way, he passed several wagons. He greeted the drivers, asking if they heard news of the shipwreck of the Liberty. If they did, he asked about Caroline Shaw and if she was one of the passengers.

The third wagon he passed had stopped under an oak tree. He pulled up beside and asked if they had news of The Liberty, and in particular, news of Caroline Shaw. A young girl called a greeting. To his surprise, she asked if he was Mr. McCord.

"Yes, ma'am," he replied.

He eyed her, wondering if she might be Miss Shaw.

"I know Caroline Shaw," the woman said.

"Is she safe?"

"Yes. She's fine. Thankfully."

"Good to hear." He felt relief.

"She'll be along soon. This is the first wagon. I left with the mothers and children," the woman replied.

Nick wasn't sure why she explained all that, but he nodded and offered what he hoped was a friendly smile. The woman whispered a few words to the rest of the group and to his dismay, they all turned their attention his way. They studied him keenly. His face warmed.

He heard their soft murmurs. *It's true. He is indeed. So remarkable.*

He frowned and regretted his decision to stop and ask about Miss Shaw.

To his annoyance, Annie had noted their peculiar behavior. She leaned against his shoulder, straining to hear the women's quiet conversation.

"What are they talking about?" she asked.

"I don't know. Never mind."

"Does she like kittens?" Annie whispered. "That Miss Shaw lady, do you think she'd like my kitten?"

"Hush," he said softly. He clasped the sleeping kitten and attempted to lift it, only to feel the claws grasp his shirt and hang on for dear life. He handed the reins to Annie and told her to hold them just for a moment so he could remove the dang cat from his shoulder. He pulled the cat higher, but it refused to release its hold on him.

"Put him back down and pet him," Annie said.

Nick, exasperated by the cat, set it down and stroked his thumb across its head. It purred and pushed into his thumb, like a cow scratching its head on a good oak. Nick cupped his hand under the kitten's front paws and lifted again, and this time the cat came easily.

As he set the cat on Annie's lap, he looked back at the women in the wagon. They all eyed him intently, and from the looks on their smiling faces, he guessed this group of ladies were the type that loved cats.

The young lady kept her gaze fixed on him. "One other thing," she said demurely, her gaze flitting to the kitten.

One other thing.

He winced inwardly. The young lady's innocent-sounding question might be trouble.

Whenever a woman wanted to ask one other thing, it rarely resulted in her asking one other thing. Usually, it meant a dozen more questions or, worse, no questions whatsoever.

"Yes?" he said cautiously.

Once more, Annie leaned closer. He wanted to nudge back, elbow her out of the entire conversation. He could tell her ears were pricked and taking in every word. All this was going to result in a heap of actual questions from a very curious little girl.

The woman spoke. "Caroline is one of the finest persons I've ever known."

He nodded. The woman spoke in earnest, and he had to respect that. He tipped his hat and prepared to take his leave. "All right. Thank you for telling me. I look forward to meeting her. Much obliged."

"You'll take good care of her, won't you?" This came from one of the other ladies on the wagon.

His heart sank. More questions he didn't want to answer. Why had he stopped? He asked himself the same question once again. By now, every woman in the back of the wagon studied him as if he were on trial for some dastardly offense.

He paused and studied the group of women. Each one had made the voyage to Texas with Caroline Shaw. He sensed their strong feelings about her, their respect and esteem. Even the wagon driver, who had presumably not made the trip with Caroline, eyed him with deep suspicion as if he too sided with Miss Shaw.

"You going to do the right thing?" the old-timer wagon driver asked.

Nick replied immediately. "Of course, I will."

The words slipped out before he'd had a chance to think. What else could he say? That he wouldn't take good care of Miss Shaw? It seemed wrong. Ungallant. Any man worth his salt prided himself on how he respected and cared for womenfolk. No, he'd make sure Caroline Shaw was safe and secure before he bid her farewell.

His answer seemed to please the young lady. She beamed. The rest of the women nodded their approval and spoke amongst themselves. In less than a minute's time, he'd been tried, judged, and deemed innocent... or, at the least, adequate.

The wagon driver, unlike his female passengers, didn't look entirely convinced of Nick's testimony. He eyed him suspiciously. Nick felt a pang of guilt but said nothing.

The driver nodded a silent, wary goodbye before continuing on his way to Galveston.

Nick set off in the other direction, continuing down the road toward the stranded passengers. A sense of unease came over him. Caroline Shaw might not be the liar and cheat that he'd imagined. This might be a little more complicated than he'd expected.

Chapter Nine
A Not-So Friendly Introduction

Caroline

Standing alone on the shore, Caroline relished the quiet and peace, a small respite from the passengers crowded round the fire. It surprised her that the captain hadn't stormed across the beach to demand she return to the group. Captain Wilson watched over his passengers much like a protective hen guarded her chicks.

Soon she'd say goodbye to him too.

A man's voice broke the quiet. "Miss Shaw?"

She looked up, expecting to find the captain or one of the ship's crew, but the man who'd spoken to her was a stranger. Tall. Imposing. He stood a dozen paces away.

"I didn't want to startle you," he said, removing his cowboy hat.

"That's kind of you."

He didn't reply but kept his gaze fixed on her as if struck by some aspect of her appearance. Probably her wild, unkempt hair. She likely looked as if she'd just washed up on the beach along with some of the ship's debris. She coaxed her lips into some semblance of a smile. "Are you one of the wagon drivers from Galveston?"

He drew near, closing the distance between them, stopping several paces away. For a long moment, he eyed her in silence.

His peculiar interest was unnerving. She'd always been told it was rude to stare. She grew flustered, unsure who he could be or why he studied her so carefully. Her attention drifted to another figure a dozen or so paces behind the stranger. A small child.

Slowly, it dawned on her. This was no stranger. Or was it? Heavens. A man traveling with a child. Surely this wasn't who she thought it was.

"Are you...?" She tried to swallow the lump in her throat.

"Nick McCord." His tone was even, resolute, as if he were reporting an official detail.

Caroline tried to coax a breath into her lungs. This was Mr. McCord. The man she'd come to marry. Her husband-to-be. "Hello, Mr. McCord."

"Hello, Caroline Shaw."

"This is a bit of a surprise."

"I'll bet."

She flinched at his reply, not just the words, but his tone. "I beg your pardon?"

Mr. McCord seemed to consider his response. Caroline couldn't begin to imagine his thoughts. Was he disappointed to come face to face with his mail-order bride? Did he find her lacking? She'd pictured this moment a hundred times, but never had she imagined her husband-to-be would be so standoffish and rude, frankly.

She recalled his letters and Beth's comments about his looks and what she assumed was his vanity. Well, Mr. McCord might be good-looking. Maybe. Perhaps under some circumstances, but his narrowed eyes and grim expression made him look more fearsome than handsome.

Then again, she hadn't come to Texas for him so much as for the girl. Her heart skipped a beat as she took in the sight of the small child.

Annie stood back some distance. She was clad in trousers and shirtsleeves, much like Mr. McCord, and to Caroline's dismay, she wore the same unfriendly expression. In her arms, she held a kitten. It watched her too, its little ears pricked forward, the only friendly look in the bunch. Caroline had the urge to turn on her heel and march back to the group of passengers.

"What I meant by surprise," Mr. McCord said, his tone slightly more amenable, "pertained to the ship hitting some rocks. Must have been a surprise."

"To be sure."

"You came to Texas as a mail-order bride." He said the words as if speaking to himself.

"That's correct," she said. Had the man been drinking? Was he the sort of man who was fond of the bottle? Heavens, she hadn't thought of asking in the various letters they'd exchanged.

"Well, I can't leave you here," he said.

Caroline blinked, wondering if she'd heard him correctly.

"The captain wants to talk to us before we leave."

He gestured toward the throng of passengers and the crew. The shipwrecked passengers and sailors stood in small groups on the sandy beach, waiting for the wagons to take them to Galveston.

Caroline began the trek back up the path. Mr. McCord walked beside her and the girl on the other side of him. Her lips turned downward with clear disapproval. "Is she coming with us?" Annie asked.

"Oh, dear," Caroline said under her breath.

"Mind your manners," Nick said.

The girl looked affronted, then wounded. Her chin trembled as her eyes filled with the suggestion of tears. Caroline felt an immediate pang of sympathy. Mr. McCord had a loud, intimidating voice. No wonder the girl felt stung by his response.

"Hello, Annie," she said gently as they walked together. "I'm Caroline Shaw."

The girl didn't reply.

"I intended to bring you a present. From Boston."

The girl shrugged wordlessly. Caroline glanced at Mr. McCord, but his face was a mask of irritation, as if fetching his mail-order bride was just another task on a long and trying list of chores. Mr. McCord was certainly no Prince Charming. She ignored his gruff demeanor and turned her attention back to the girl.

"Unfortunately, my gift is sitting at the bottom of the Gulf of Mexico. Along with the fish. My baggage sank with the ship," she added with a grim cheerfulness. "So, I'm traveling light. In case you're wondering."

This got a reaction from the ill-humored McCords. Both regarded her with a fleeting interest, which passed as quickly as it came. Only the kitten showed dismay, or so it seemed, judging by the mournful mew. Annie spoke softly, trying to soothe the animal, but soon it began mewing in earnest.

"Is your kitten hungry?" Caroline asked.

"No," Annie replied.

"No, *ma'am*," Nick corrected.

"No, ma'am," Annie muttered.

As they approached the group of passengers, Caroline spotted the captain on the far side of the crowd. He came to speak to them, a stern frown etched on his brow.

"I've met Mr. McCord and will agree to your leaving with him."

"Glad I meet your approval," Mr. McCord remarked.

"On one condition," the captain added.

Nick turned to Caroline with a look of silent inquiry. He seemed to think she and the captain were in some sort of conspiracy together. Caroline couldn't imagine what the captain expected of her or of Nick.

"What's the condition, Captain Wilson?" she asked.

"I assume your husband-to-be has honorable intentions."

Mr. McCord grumbled.

Caroline tried her best to ignore his rough manners. Perhaps he'd improve with some gentle instruction, just like the girl. She straightened her shoulders, doubling her resolve.

"Of course, his intentions are honorable," Caroline said. "I have complete faith in him."

"I did not realize he was a *bounty hunter*," the captain said.

Caroline wanted to point out that she was the one marrying Mr. McCord. It hardly mattered what the captain knew or didn't know. Now was not the time to make a fuss about her arrangements.

"He's a fine, upstanding man," Caroline said quietly.

The captain furrowed his brows. "That may well be. Just the same, I insist the two of you exchange vows. Before nightfall."

Chapter Ten
Nick Falls Ill

Nick

Nick had every intention of speaking candidly to Caroline Shaw. To tell her everything, or at least what he knew. But something about seeing her on the beach softened his heart. In that instant, he knew Caroline would be the type of woman who would care for Annie if anything were to happen to him. With that thought in mind, his indignation faded.

What it was that changed his heart, he couldn't say exactly. He liked to think he was a good judge of character. Perhaps it was her eyes, or the way he'd found her in prayer. Something peculiar had come over him in the moment when he first glimpsed the girl, her head bowed, a lonely figure on a deserted shore.

The sight moved him. It was so much like the dream he'd had a few days ago. Then again, maybe the wound on his arm was beginning to fester and muddle his thoughts. With each passing hour, the pesky cut was paining him a tad more.

They bid the captain farewell. Nick ushered the girls to the wagon and helped them aboard. Caroline seemed reluctant to accept his help but relented.

They made the trip back to Galveston in an awkward silence. Annie kept giving him a quizzical look as if to ask what he intended to do. He intended to do just what the captain had asked. He had to admit he was as surprised as anyone. His plan was turning out far different than what he intended, but his heart told him it was the right way.

Two hours later they arrived back at the Hotel Rebecca. Caroline, who'd been quiet as a mouse, took charge of matters. She started when the hotel clerk made a fuss about Annie's kitten. Caroline promised to watch the kitten and make sure it didn't cause mischief. She lowered her voice so that Annie wouldn't hear and went on to explain that Annie hadn't ever known her mother or father and did they want to cause the poor child more distress.

Nick was starting to feel lightheaded from the pain in his arm. His wound throbbed. The pain radiated clear all the way up to his shoulder. Still, he had enough of his wits about him to notice and admire Caroline's business-like demeanor. Getting shipwrecked hadn't seemed to trouble her much. She was pretty too, especially when she was all fired up about the pesky kitten.

She was middling height. Her hair was a mass of chocolate-colored curls that sprang every which way. The curls framed her face, drawing his eye to her soft skin. He probably stared at her like a poor, lovesick boy.

He had to wonder how Caroline knew of Annie's circumstances. Whoever sent off for a mail-order bride must have explained matters. What else did Caroline know? Likely more about him than he did about her after reading a single letter.

His head was beginning to ache, so he resolved to think about the matter some other time. Meanwhile, he needed to make certain to abide by the captain's wishes. Somewhere between the shipwreck and Galveston, he'd changed his mind about everything.

They trudged upstairs.

"I'm feeling a mite poorly," he muttered when they returned to the room.

"You look terrible," Annie said as she stroked her kitten's head.

Caroline stood by the door, her face pale and drawn. A moment before, she'd been giving the hotel clerk an earful. Her bravado had vanished somewhere along the stairwell.

"I'm not entirely comfortable entering a gentleman's hotel room. I'd ask for my own accommodations if I had the means to pay."

Her voice trembled and Nick felt a stab of sympathy. He still wasn't entirely sure if Caroline Shaw was as innocent as she let on. What if she was in cahoots with the Bethany Springs matchmaker? But he had to admit, she'd been through a trying ordeal. Even if she was a conniving woman, she hadn't deserved to get shipwrecked. Maybe she'd been praying for God's forgiveness when he first saw her on the shore.

"No need to fret, Miss Shaw. I'll send for a justice of the peace to do the honors. And some supper for the three of us."

Supper arrived before the local JP, but Nick wasn't a bit hungry. By the time the official knocked on the door, Nick was beginning to feel feverish. The gentleman made a fuss over Caroline, asking her a dozen questions about her coming to Texas as a mail-order bride. Did she enter into marriage willingly and so on. Sweat trickled down the back of Nick's neck.

Caroline answered all his questions, assuring him she'd come of her own accord. She was ready to enter into marriage freely and willingly. Her tone was firm, even resolute.

With that, the justice of the peace invited them to exchange vows. Annie stood off to the side, holding her kitten and watching with wide eyes. The child might not have wanted a stepmother, but she'd come around soon enough. Nick had a gut feeling, one that never steered him wrong.

He managed to say his vows, sign the ledger, and pay the man for his service. When the fellow left, Nick took his leave, muttering a few words about not feeling himself. He trudged off to bed. As he closed his eyes and sank into sleep, he wondered if he was having a dream, a not unpleasant dream, but a mighty peculiar one to be sure.

Here and there, he awoke briefly to find Caroline at his bedside eyeing him studiously along with Annie who peered at him with deep concern.

"Your uncle is a stubborn man," Caroline said gently.

He tried to object but no words came out.

"Yes, ma'am," Annie replied.

A moment later, he felt a tug on his sleeve and heard the tear of material.

"Hey now," he grumbled.

Next came the sting of medicine.

He growled.

"Oh, hush," Caroline said softly. "Surely a legendary bounty hunter from Texas can tolerate a little antiseptic."

"He's not very brave," Annie commented. "Not when he's hurt."

"Is that so?" Caroline's voice held an edge of amusement.

If he'd felt up to it, he'd have given both of them a piece of his mind. Of course, he was brave. And why was Caroline acting like any of this was amusing? What kind of woman had he married? A pretty one, but she might not be as tenderhearted as he'd imagined.

"He's real bad about splinters," Annie said. "When he was putting up fences on Uncle Theo's back pastures, he'd bellyache every night about splinters."

That little turncoat. Talking about him like he wasn't right there.

Caroline laughed softly as she tugged off his boots and spread a blanket over him. He relished the warmth and comfort. He ached all over, not just where he'd gotten slashed by the thief's knife. He couldn't help feeling a tad resentful. Neither Caroline nor Annie seemed particularly concerned about his plight, making jokes about his tolerance for pain and whatnot. He'd like to point out that he was as tough as they came. Tougher.

Someone, likely Caroline, put out the lamp. His vision darkened.

"I reckon bounty hunters don't have to contend with many splinters," Annie said thoughtfully.

"Indeed," Caroline murmured.

Nick tried to reply but couldn't summon the strength. Instead, he sank into the bed and considered Caroline's lovely tresses. He fell asleep wondering if they were as soft and delicate as they appeared.

Chapter Eleven
Nick is Unsufferable

Caroline

Sleeping fitfully, Caroline woke every short while to check on Nick. She and Annie slept in the smaller bedroom down a short hallway. The girl seemed a tad standoffish at times. When Caroline tried to help her settle in for the evening, she'd grown decidedly obstinate, claiming she wasn't a baby and didn't need to be fussed over.

Caroline resolved to ignore the girl's impudence. She didn't care for Annie's tone, but when the time was right, she'd offer gentle instruction to the child.

Nick slept fitfully as well. Each time she checked on him, the bedding had been tossed aside. She tried to cover him with a blanket in case his fever returned, but to no avail.

She awoke with the first glimmers of dawn. The sound of footsteps drew her from sleep. In an instant, she was on her feet, hurrying down the hallway. As she rounded the corner, she stopped abruptly. Nick stood a few paces away. Shadows darkened his features, and with his looming height, Caroline couldn't hold back a startled cry.

"Oh, it's you," he grumbled.

She drew a sharp breath of surprise. While Nick McCord wasn't exactly the warmest ray of sunshine, she liked to imagine she'd earned a friendlier greeting. She'd tended to him all night long and he couldn't even manage a good morning.

"Lovely to see you this morning," she replied.

"You're wearing the same dress as yesterday."

"The rest of my dresses sank with my trunks."

"That's right."

"Or perhaps they're floating. I'm not certain. The only thing I know for sure is that I must take good care of this dress."

He scrubbed a hand down his face and muttered. Why that was, she couldn't say. It wasn't as if all his worldly possessions had been lost at sea.

"We'd best get you some new..." He gestured as he tried to find the proper words. "Frocks and whatnot. Shoes and whatever a lady might need."

"Perhaps I can purchase some material. Nothing fancy, of course."

"Won't that take time? For you to sew a bunch of dresses?"

"Not too long. I'm not as proficient at dressmaking as cooking, but I'll manage."

"You know how to cook?"

"I do. You might recall I told you that in my first letter. And my fourth letter as well. When I turned eighteen, I left the orphanage to work at the boarding house a few doors down."

"Sorry." He cleared his throat. "I reckon I forgot."

"Did you actually *read* any of my letters?"

It took him a moment to reply. Caroline's heart sank. How she'd agonized about those letters to Nick and after all that, he didn't remember anything about her. It was as if she were a stranger to him. The notion he'd simply discarded the letters sent a stab of pain across her heart.

"Look at us," he drawled. "We've been man and wife for less than a day, and we're already having our first quarrel."

The kitten padded down the hallway, mewing plaintively. A moment later, Annie appeared, her hair mussed from sleep. She mumbled a few groggy words, picked up the kitten and returned to her bed.

"Annie's not an early riser. Not like me," Nick said. "After breakfast, we'll visit some of the dress shops along the Strand. I'm not taking you home looking like you just washed up on the beach without so much as a spare dress or pair of shoes."

He chuckled. "Which is pretty much the fact of the matter."

The man was insufferable. Impossible. He scarcely even bothered to smile but had no trouble making light of her circumstances.

Chapter Twelve
Uncle Theo's Ranch

Nick

Shopping for Caroline's provisions agreed with him more than he expected. While she'd argued about buying anything but the barest essentials, he'd won her over eventually. His mind was still trying to make sense of his circumstances. He hadn't expected to return to Bethany Springs with a wife. He'd always imagined he'd find one eventually, just not like this.

Someone or some people had conspired to marry him off. He couldn't imagine who, but ever since meeting Caroline, he cared less and less. He'd gone from tolerating the notion to appreciating her company. She had a quick mind, a strong but kind character. She'd arrived in Texas less than a day before and already had shown her mettle.

When they reached Bethany Springs and Theo's home came into view, Nick couldn't resist stealing a few glimpses of Caroline. She sat beside him on the buckboard bench, Annie riding between them. Caroline had changed out of her bedraggled dress, thank goodness, and wore a pale blue frock with lace trim. He thought she looked prettier each time he glanced her way.

"What do you think?" he asked as he stopped the team.

"It's lovely. Even nicer than the sketch you sent me."

Annie snickered. He shot her a warning look. Back in Galveston, he'd promised her a puppy to go with the new kitten. All she had to do was keep her lips buttoned, not a word about the mystery matchmakers. Or the letters he hadn't written.

"Your Uncle Theo must have been a peculiar man," she said. "To stipulate that someone can inherit a ranch, this beautiful ranch and homestead, simply by naming a son after him... that's unusual, to say the least."

"Yeah, I reckon it is." Nick wondered how much Caroline knew about him and his family, a lot more than he knew about her, that much was certain.

"And your cousins asking you to raise Annie here... what a blessing for you and her."

She knew that too... "Yes, it is a blessing."

Nick realized he needed to tread lightly. Hopefully, he wouldn't contradict any of the details the matchmakers had shared. He wasn't used to guarding his thoughts. As a lawman, he'd been more used to people trying to outwit him, not the other way around.

One day, when Caroline was a little more settled, he'd come clean. Until then, he'd have to be careful. More than anything, he wanted to make her feel welcome and appreciated.

"I would think they wouldn't want to part with such a fine home and ranch land."

"Well, technically, they haven't parted with anything. All three of my cousins would like to own this ranch, but they have their own houses now, and they refuse to name a son Theodore just because our crazy uncle wanted them to. My Uncle Wade knows more about the legal aspects of who owns this land right now... I don't own it, and I'm not sure who does honestly, but if I can find a way, I intend to buy it, because it's the prettiest place I've ever seen."

Nick wasn't much of a conversationalist, but for some reason he had plenty to say to Caroline about this ranch. He hadn't given it much thought up to now, but now that he was married, he realized that he needed a home that was permanent, a home where he and his wife could raise their girl, Annie.

He held his breath, hoping that his comments matched what she'd read in the letters. Thankfully, she responded with a sweet smile as she studied the expanse of rugged ranch land.

"It's a little rough and needs work," he admitted. "Theo neglected it for some time. But I intend to make something of the good Lord's providence."

Her eyes lit up as she gazed into his. For a moment, neither spoke. The kitten interrupted the sweet moment with her plaintive mewing.

"We'd best get everyone home," he said gruffly.

"Someone's getting hungry." Caroline stroked the kitten's head.

When they reached the house, he helped her down and ushered her inside.

"It's a little sparse," he said. "I been meaning to get some curtains."

Caroline wandered through the front room, taking in the details. "It's very nice. Bigger than I expected."

She stood in the middle of what ought to have been a sitting room. Or what *might* be a sitting room one day when it had a few proper chairs, a comfortable chesterfield for folks to actually sit on. A smile played upon her lips. As she walked the perimeter of the room, her footsteps echoed across the floorboards.

"Uncle Theo was a bachelor," Nick said, trying to explain. "He didn't worry too much about furniture, or silverware, or curtains."

"Your letters made it very clear that he was an eccentric man."

Letters. He winced. "We'll get some nicer furniture first thing."

Annie wandered to the doorway. "I thought we were getting a puppy first thing."

"Sounds like you're starting a list," he said, narrowing his eyes at Annie.

The girl's expression brightened. "Can I add a pony?"

He arched a brow.

All along, Annie had complained about the possibility he might one day marry. Now that he'd gone ahead and done just that, he'd have to watch the two girls. They might join forces. If Annie had her way, she'd have an entire zoo living there on the ranch. And if Caroline had her way, well... who could say?

He suppressed a smile despite the notion of being outnumbered. If he'd let his pride rule his heart, he might have spoken up. Loudly. But no. He'd rather contend with the two girls teaming up than the two of them at odds. He'd never spent much time imagining a peaceful home life. Not till Aunt Penny named him in her will, along with the stipulation that he care for Annie.

Everything changed when he first learned of Aunt Penny's hopes for him and Annie. It all somehow brought him to the Texas shore, just the day prior. Who could say what the Lord had in mind. Sometimes He answered prayers before they were even whispered. Maybe there was hope for the three of them to come together and form a patchwork family. One day.

Chapter Thirteen
Nick's Confession

Caroline

Their first evening at home, they ate a simple dinner of ham sandwiches made from the provisions they'd picked up earlier that day. It seemed a meager meal to serve her new family. Caroline felt a twinge of dismay and silently vowed to do better for Nick and Annie as time went on.

They chatted during the meal. For the most part, the conversation flowed easily with only occasional awkward lapses. Caroline asked how his injured arm was faring. He dismissed her concerns but thanked her for tending to him.

"You likely didn't expect to play nursemaid right after getting hitched," he joked.

"I was happy to help. Growing up in an orphanage meant doing any number of tasks. We studied reading, writing and arithmetic but also on the matter of duty, contributing to the general good. All of us girls pitched in as best we could."

"That's how you learned all about cooking and tending to folks when they got injured," Nick offered.

"Yes."

"Were the people unkind?" Annie asked.

"Unkind?" Caroline shook her head. "No. The orphanage was headed by a Methodist church minister and run by a group of elderly ladies. They were strict. Certainly. But kind."

Annie eyed her with a skeptical look. "Did you have enough to eat?"

"Of course." Caroline suppressed a smile.

"Did they feed you gruel?"

"Gruel?" Caroline blinked. "What do you mean?"

Annie gazed at her wide-eyed. "Like they fed the orphans in *Oliver Twist*? Did you have to ask for more when you were hungry?"

"I can assure you that I never once ate gruel while I was growing up."

Annie frowned, unconvinced.

"I never went hungry. The food they prepared in the kitchens came from parishioner's farms. We had eggs every morning for breakfast, often with fried potatoes, ham, and freshly baked bread. They didn't serve gruel. Not for breakfast, lunch, or dinner."

Annie didn't reply, still looking doubtful.

"Someone's read a little too much Charles Dickens," Caroline said with a smile.

"Aunt Penny was a librarian," Nick explained. "She always read heaps of books to Annie."

The girl grew pensive. Her eyes took on a sad, faraway look at the mention of her Aunt Penny. Caroline wished she could ease some of the girl's sadness. Perhaps Annie would allow her to read to her as time went on. Perhaps something happier than *Oliver Twist*.

"I think I would have liked your Aunt Penny," Caroline said gently.

Annie nodded but remained silent and thoughtful. She seemed to have lost her appetite and didn't eat much more of her supper. After their meal, Annie helped clear the dishes before doing her evening chores.

Caroline watched her set off down the trail to the barn with the small, still nameless kitten bounding behind her.

"I reckon we ought to discuss where you'll bed down tonight," Nick offered a bland smile as he filled the dishpan from a nearby bucket.

Caroline averted her eyes, hardly able to meet his gaze. Ever since she'd set sail on the Liberty, she'd agonized over various aspects of marriage. "Well..." she said, her voice drifting off.

"There's no need to fret," Nick said with a hint of amusement.

Caroline was too overcome to reply to his teasing tone. One thing was certain: Texans were more direct in their speech. A Boston fellow would have taken his time before broaching such a delicate subject.

"I'm not f-fretting."

Heat rose to her face. She was fretting. Clearly. To his credit, Nick didn't tease or provoke her or even notice her nervous stammering. She kept her gaze averted as she began washing cups.

Nick leaned against the counter. "I have an extra bed up in the barn. I'll haul it down and set it up in the back room and sleep there. You can take my room."

She stopped her task. "I don't want to take your room. Why not give me the back room?"

They argued back and forth as Caroline washed and rinsed the dishes. He took each dish from her, dried and stacked them. The work was done quickly, and the amiable debate calmed her nerves.

"I want you to have a more comfortable bed," he said with a tone of finality.

With that, he peered out the window. "Dang. Well, that didn't take long."

Caroline followed his gaze. A horse-drawn wagon crested the distant hill. It moved at a good clip. Clouds of dust billowed in its wake. A moment later, Annie burst into the house, shouting with excitement. "Aunt Sophie's on her way. Uncle Robert too."

Caroline smiled with a rush of happiness. She'd heard so much about Sophie and Robert. Indeed. It seemed she already knew them.

Nick spoke. "My aunt and uncle have helped me more than I care to admit."

"I seem to recall."

"They're always offering to help out. When I try to pay them back, they like to make the same joke."

"They say they'll put it on your bill," Caroline said with a smile. "I recall that too."

Nick gazed at her for a long moment. She'd thought the McCords' comment was charming and humorous, but he seemed somber.

"I reckon I ought to tell you something else," he said.

"Sophie and Robert aren't really your aunt and uncle? They're distant cousins."

"No, not that."

"That Sophie loves to cook and will insist on feeding us at least once a week, if not more. Especially after the fall roundup."

He grimaced. "Not that either."

"That Sophie has a temper?"

He raked his fingers through his hair and gazed out the window for a long moment. Sophie and Robert would arrive shortly. Caroline wondered what on earth had left Nick so pensive and quiet.

Finally, he spoke. "Sophie and Robert might not know I've taken a wife."

"They might not know?"

He shrugged. "Or they might know everything. I can't rightly say."

His words made no sense. His aunt and uncle might know nothing, or they might know everything. "I'm sorry. I don't understand."

"I ought to have confessed something right from the beginning."

"You mean when you first wrote me?"

He stole a glance at her before peering back out the window at the McCord wagon as it came down the road. He cleared his throat, scratched the back of his neck and finally, after what seemed an endless wait, he began to speak. "Those letters you got. From me."

"Yes," she said softly.

"Up in Baltimore."

"Baltimore?"

He knit his brow. "Where did you live?"

"Where did I live?"

"Before you came to Texas."

"I lived in Boston."

"Right."

Her confusion grew. What on earth? How had he forgotten such an important part of her life? She'd been born and raised in one single town. Boston. How was it possible that he seemed not to recall or didn't know?

And yet... he seemed not to know. Her skin prickled. Her throat felt dry and tight. She spoke, doing her best to keep an even, calm tone. "What about the letters? What did you mean to tell me in the beginning?"

"You see." He looked her square in the eye. "I never wrote them."

Her heart thudded. "You," her voice dulled to a soft whisper. "You never wrote the letters that I received?"

He shook his head and reached a hand for hers. She yanked her hand back and retreated several steps. "Are you saying you didn't write those letters?"

"I didn't," he said quietly. "I don't know who wrote them."

Her mind swirled with a hundred frightening thoughts. The letters she'd read a hundred times over and over hadn't even been written by Nick McCord. The man she'd just yesterday agreed to honor and obey. Who was this man? Her husband. Who had she married?

"Don't be afraid, Caroline."

"I'm too astonished to be afraid," she whispered. "Should I be afraid?"

He looked her square in the eye. "No."

"Forgive me if I'm unconvinced," she said softly.

He shook his head and folded his arms across his chest. "I swore to the judge in Galveston to honor and protect. I'm a decent man, God-fearing and hardworking. I will be a good man for you. I didn't write those letters, but I might be able to guess who did."

"Dear heavens. Of all the difficulties I imagined, I never once imagined someone other than you wrote those letters."

"Please don't fret."

She gave a breathless laugh. Her knees felt like they might give way beneath her. She could hardly draw a proper breath and Nick was suggesting she not fret.

He scratched his jaw. "I wonder who wrote the letters."

She wasn't sure if she cared. At this point it hardly mattered. And yet, she found herself considering the mysterious question. The wagon approached the house. Any moment, Sophie and Robert McCord would arrive.

"You think it was your Aunt Sophie?"

"If only you still had them so that I could take a look. Sophie? Maybe." He pressed his lips together and had the decency to look abashed. "Could have been Aunt Amelia."

"*Could* have been?" Her voice sounded shrill, but she couldn't help herself.

He grew thoughtful. "Or Molly, Daniel's husband. She's been after me ever since I got to Bethany Springs."

The sound of the nearby wagon stirred Caroline from her turmoil. Robert McCord spoke to his team as they stopped before the house. He set the brake and hitched the animals to the post. As he circled the wagon, Sophie fussed at him about the dust he'd stirred up on the road. He dismissed her comments with a laugh as he lifted her down from the wagon.

Caroline watched the scene with a vague sense of disbelief. Was she dreaming? No. This was all very real and so much worse than anything she'd imagined as she traveled to Texas.

In a moment, she'd meet a couple she'd heard so much about. How many times had she pictured Sophie McCord? And Amelia Honeycutt. Now she wondered if Aunt Sophie had written the letters. Or was it Amelia who had penned the letters?

"We'll find out who wrote to you," Nick said, stirring her from her thoughts, his tone resolute. "First thing. I'll ask and get to the bottom of this."

"Nick," she whispered. "Whatever you do, please don't ask your aunt if she sent for me."

He frowned. "Don't you want to know?"

Did she want to know? Very much. And yet, she found the idea humiliating. She couldn't bear the thought of Nick asking people if they'd written to her. How many people would he need to ask. One? Two. Twenty? She cringed with a scorching sense of shame.

"Not yet." She gulped. "Please don't ask. Not now. I'm still too shocked. And mortified."

Nick might have had the decency to show some sympathy. Instead, his lips curved into a broad smile. He might have been surprised by the events of the past few days, but clearly, he wasn't mortified. Not a bit.

"Don't you worry, Caroline. I hadn't intended on getting a missus, but you're a sight better than anything I could have hoped for."

Caroline had no reply. It all seemed too hard to grasp. Nick hadn't sent for her. A stranger had written the letters.

Beth had been the first to suggest this very thing. It seemed so long ago. She recalled the moment Beth had asked what at the time seemed an absurd question. She'd spied the adornments on the margins of the letter, small decorative hearts and scrolls.

I suspect your husband-to-be, Nick McCord, didn't write these letters.

Caroline had promptly dismissed Beth's absurd notions. Now she knew the painful truth. It had all been a lie.

She eyed her husband. He was gentle, and so far, he seemed kind. Very kind. She appreciated that aspect of her new husband. To his credit, he doted on Annie. He seemed eager to welcome Caroline to his home and into his life despite his prior reluctance to marry. What had changed, she had to wonder.

To her bewilderment, he found this entire matter somewhat amusing. A smile tugged at his lips. "Missus," he murmured with bemusement. "Mrs. McCord. What a notion."

She wiped her hands on a dishrag and ran her palms across her skirt, preparing to meet Sophie and Robert McCord. Hopefully, she looked somewhat presentable.

Following Nick to the front door, her thoughts swirled. Dear heaven above. How had she landed herself so far outside of the proverbial frying pan and right into the flames of a Texas fire?

Chapter Fourteen
Dances with Girls

Nick

If Aunt Sophie was the matchmaking culprit, she certainly put on a good show of innocence. She and Robert made a big fuss over Caroline and acted mighty pleased for the two of them. They insisted they wouldn't stay too long, just enough time to say hello, drop off several cuts of beef from the McCord ranch and some books for Annie.

He didn't get too many visitors lately due to the fall roundup. The McCords and the Honeycutts were busy from dawn till way past dusk. For the next few weeks, he and Caroline would be left to themselves, which might be a good thing, depending on how you looked at it. Nick wasn't entirely sure that Caroline would like the big, boisterous McCord and Honeycutt families. A little extra time to settle in might better prepare her for that sort of meeting. A little extra time might help. They'd be alone, and they'd really get to know each other. He hoped that would be good for both of them.

"I'm sure Caroline is exhausted after her journey," Sophie said.

She eyed Caroline, his new wife, with unabashed curiosity. *New wife.* How peculiar that phrase sounded in his mind. And yet so very pleasing. Caroline was more than he could have imagined. As much as he doubted the notion of love at first sight, he might become a believer.

"I'm feeling well enough, thank you," Caroline replied shyly.

Nick had to admire how well she'd managed to compose herself in light of his confession. She looked a tad pale. No wonder Sophie thought she was exhausted. More likely, his mail-order bride was reeling from learning she had come all the way to Texas to marry a stranger. One who hadn't sent for her.

"We must have a party," Sophie announced. "To celebrate."

"Sounds like a fine idea," Robert said, beaming at the two of them before turning his attention to Nick. "I must admit, I didn't expect you to settle down anytime soon."

"Are you surprised?" Nick eyed Sophie, wondering if she might give herself away. There were a number of busybodies in Bethany Springs, but Sophie McCord might be the busiest of them all.

"Of course," Sophie replied. "You never seemed the least bit interested in a wife."

"Is that so?" Caroline asked, turning to face him. "You were reluctant?"

Nick chuckled at her question. She had no idea how reluctant. Or maybe she was beginning to understand.

"He was too picky," Sophie grumbled. "I tried to help him find a nice girl."

"Really?" Caroline said pointedly. "But there wasn't a nice girl available? Or what happened?"

Nick had to smile inwardly.

Sophie continued. If she sensed Caroline's discomfort, she gave no sign. "I had a party," Sophie explained. "I served a nice meal and invited all the eligible young ladies from five counties. We had a fine time and Nick even agreed to dance with a few of the young ladies, but afterward he complained. This girl was too tall. That girl was too short. The other was too bossy."

Caroline listened attentively. He wondered if she might pepper him with questions later, after his aunt and uncle left.

Meanwhile Annie grinned at Sophie's animated telling of the story. She had her own opinions to add. "Uncle Nick was like Goldilocks. Not too tall. Not too short. Looking for a wife that was just right."

They laughed. Even Nick. The only one who refrained was Caroline, who remained quiet as her face turned pink. To Nick's thinking, her blush made her even prettier.

Nick recalled the party Sophie had hosted. He'd had more reasons for dismissing the various young ladies. Reasons that had little to do with their height or appearance. His reasons went far deeper.

Sophie and Robert didn't linger. Robert asked a few questions about the ranch and the number of cattle Nick had acquired. The herd was small. Nick had to admit as much but all that would change soon. Nick might be a newcomer to ranching, but he was determined to learn and grow his enterprise. Robert didn't give him too much ribbing, not like the rest of the McCord clan. Darn them. The Honeycutt brothers weren't much better when it came to poking fun at a bounty hunter turned rancher.

After a short visit, short by McCord standards, Robert and Sophie said their good-byes and departed.

That evening, he and Annie went about their usual bedtime routine. The girl washed up, got into her nightgown, and headed to bed. He met her at the doorway. She yawned, and everything about her suggested she was more than ready for sleep.

She knelt on the small rug beside the bed. He knelt beside her as he did each evening. They joined hands and prayed. Annie always started off the prayer by thanking God for His blessings that day. Nick wasn't entirely surprised that most of her thanks pertained to the kitten.

That danged kitten. Later, when he offered his own prayer, none would include a pesky critter like the one curled at Annie's side. How had he been hoodwinked into paying good money for a stray kitten? Because of Annie. That was the only possible reason.

Nick gave thanks for their safe journey home from Galveston. He also gave thanks for Caroline and her nursing skills. His arm needed a few more days to heal properly, but he knew it would be fine. The fever and pain were gone. The incident at the harbor was just a fading memory.

"Lord, I thank you for your blessings and providence." Providence. Hadn't that been the turn in the road? The unexpected source of grace? Both for him and the small girl kneeling beside him. Suddenly overcome, he drew a fortifying breath. "And for my family."

He wasn't sure if Caroline could hear them, but, of course, Nick wasn't saying the prayer for her sake. His prayers were meant for someone else entirely. He meant every word and felt them deep down in his heart. Ever since he'd taken Annie in, he'd come to appreciate the way God continued to bless him and the girl. Just a few days ago, Nick hadn't given marriage much thought. And yet...

The moment he'd met Caroline on the desolate beach, he'd understood the rightness of it all.

Sometimes the plans of any single person don't amount to the *right* plans.

After he kissed Annie good night, he found Caroline at the kitchen table, her head bent over a letter. She lifted her gaze to meet his and, to Nick's surprise, her eyes shone with tears.

She spoke, her voice choked with emotion. "I'm writing the ladies who ran the orphanage where I grew up. They insisted that I send word once I got to Texas and was married."

"Why are you upset?" he asked.

He expected a certain response, one pertaining to the mysterious letters and how she'd been deceived. That he would have understood. To his surprise, she had a different reply.

"I'm not upset. I was moved by the sight of you with Annie."

"All right." He wasn't sure if this was good news or not.

"Do you pray with her every night?" she asked softly, setting down her pen.

"Of course."

"Not just when you return from a trip?"

He took the chair opposite hers. "Every night. That's what my folks always did, so I figured it was the thing to do."

She nodded and gave a wistful smile.

"I'm not much of a family man." He reached across the table to touch her hand. He was only vaguely aware of his own gesture, but when she startled, he withdrew and folded his hands in front of him.

"I hope to learn, though," he added, trying to sound lighthearted.

"I think you're doing an admirable job."

He appreciated her praise. More than he expected or could explain. Now, if only she'd let him touch her hand. That would please him more than he cared to admit.

"Caroline, I reckon we need to get to know each other a little better. We ought to take our time. Given the circumstances."

She flushed a pretty pink. Neither spoke for a long moment. Tension stretched between them, both of them not willing to broach the subject of family, marriage or living as man and wife. Nick didn't want to rush the topic. All of it was so new. So unexpected. For both of them. He sensed her reluctance and understood. Heck, he was bewildered by the situation too.

When he'd traveled to Galveston, he'd been pretty hot under the collar. All the way to Galveston, he'd imagined breaking things off with whatever mail-order bride someone had summoned. He was prepared to put an end to the entire scheme. Until the moment he saw Caroline. In that single moment, Caroline's gentle, feminine demeanor won him over so quickly, he was still a little surprised.

Surprised. But happy. Somehow.

Setting his thoughts aside, he went on. "You didn't grow up saying bedtime prayers? Goodness. I'm a bit taken aback," he teased gently. "I thought the orphanage was run by the church."

She smiled, probably grateful for the change in subject. "We prayed morning, noon and night."

"Sounds like a lot. But I suppose that's a fine thing. To be expected with a passel of orphaned girls all under one roof."

He winced, thinking about Annie, sleeping just down the hall. How close had the girl come to joining an orphanage? If need be, the McCord family might have taken her in, but then again, it was impossible to say. It was a bridge he hoped never to cross, part of the reason he was grateful to have a wife.

Caroline met his solemn gaze. "We prayed regularly, but no one knelt beside our bed to pray with us. There were thirty girls *under one roof*." She smiled. "We were very well provided for, but we were expected to take care of ourselves. Including taking care of our regular prayers. So, I always prayed alone."

He shook his head.

"On the bright side," she added cheerfully, "I never ate gruel."

She tried to make light of the matter but, just the same, a pang of sympathy struck his heart. She'd missed out, in his opinion. If he could find a way to make up for what she'd lost, he would in a heartbeat. One thing for sure, once they got better acquainted, he'd invite her to pray with him. It seemed like a man and wife ought to share that sort of closeness.

She noted his sympathetic expression and gave a dismissive gesture. "My childhood was happy enough. We received a solid education. I didn't lack for anything."

Sure sounded like she'd missed out on one or two things. Maybe more. It gave him a peculiar sort of ache just thinking about Caroline as a young girl, growing up without a lot of attention or affection.

She went on, her voice sounding more businesslike. "I had everything I could have needed. I must confess, however, I never learned to dance."

Nick frowned, wondering why she'd mention the topic of dancing.

She gave him a pointed look, a smile playing upon her lips. "Not like all the young ladies Sophie invited for you to meet."

He nodded. "Those ladies."

"Those ladies. Yes." She gave him a prim look. "This is the first I'm hearing of parties held in the interest of marrying you off."

He suppressed a grin. Caroline's comment pleased him. She wasn't fond of him dancing with a troop of possible brides. Well, he hadn't been fond of the notion either.

"Some were too tall?" she asked.

"Some," he replied.

"Some?"

"Except for the ones who were too short."

"I see," she replied, her tone a tad cool.

He smiled, rested his chin in his hand and studied her for a long moment. "If I didn't know better, I'd say you're a mite jealous."

"Don't be absurd. How could I be jealous?" The lovely pink color returned to her face just as it had earlier. "I'm not."

"All right. If you say so."

"I say so."

"Do you like to dance?" he asked.

"I don't know how."

She sounded wistful. He steered the discussion away from the topic. "There was another reason I didn't care for any of those ladies."

She said nothing, watching him with keen interest. Her eyes were focused. Her lips pressed together with what sure looked to him like she was a mite jealous. He suppressed a gleeful smile. It wasn't right to gloat and yet part of him relished her response. He wanted her to want him all to herself because he felt just the same.

He spoke quietly this time with an earnest tone. "The other reason was something I didn't want to say in front of Annie."

"Go on."

"Every one of those ladies seemed to think Annie, a girl I consider my daughter, would be a burden."

She recoiled. "That's awful."

"Now, I never yearned to become a family man, but as soon as I started caring for Annie, I appreciated the rightness of it. Like she filled a spot I hadn't noticed was empty."

The instant he said the words, he sensed how clumsy they sounded. It was true. Taking care of Annie was the answer to his unspoken prayers. Caroline grew thoughtful. He was thankful she didn't make light of his sentiment. Instead, her expression softened, as if she found his words meaningful. Somehow, he knew she'd see things the same way he did. Somehow, he'd found a wife who would fight for the same things he wanted. A wife he hadn't planned for. He'd try his best to be the husband she yearned for. Whatever that meant.

Silence stretched between them.

In the quiet, the urge to reach for her hand came over him. Again. This time he resisted the desire. Instead, he spoke gently. "I reckon I'll need to teach you to dance one day, Caroline."

Her smile faded. She straightened her shoulders into a stiff posture as if she was sore at him for suggesting such a thing.

"No thank you," she said firmly. "I don't care to dance."

"You don't care to dance?" he asked with disbelief.

"No."

"How do you know, if you've never tried?"

She lifted her chin. "I know. And I'm certain that it's not for me."

He knew better than to press the matter. Still, he couldn't help a sense of disappointment. How could he woo or charm his unexpected bride if she resisted his attempts to grow close?

Earlier, they'd shared a tender moment. Now it was gone. How had he managed to upset her in such a short space of time? Did she have something against dancing? Or did she object to his touch and being held in his arms? Either way, he vowed to win her over. He'd find a way to get past her stubborn defenses. After all, a man ought to be able to dance with his sweet mail-order bride.

Chapter Fifteen
Annie's Defiance, Nick's Blessings

Caroline

The first morning in her new Texas home, Caroline woke just after dawn. She'd imagined this first day and how she'd cook a fine meal to impress her new husband. But no. To her dismay, Nick had already made breakfast, not just for himself but for the three of them. He dismissed her worries about oversleeping, saying he was glad she'd rested, especially after the past few days. After breakfast, he and Annie left to tend to the horses down at the barn, leaving her to explore the house.

The sunshiny kitchen, situated in the corner of the ranch house, boasted a pantry that was bigger than any Caroline had ever seen, even in the orphanage. Behind the heavy oak door, she discovered rows and rows of canned goods, jars brimming with crimson tomatoes, spice-scented fruits, and a half-dozen varieties of pickles.

A root cellar just a few steps from the kitchen door and down a dozen steps stored crates overflowing with turnips, potatoes, and carrots. She wandered around the small dark room, making out the contents amidst the dim shadows. Spiderwebs hung across the cellar. She brushed them aside, shuddering at the unpleasant sensation.

After surveying the cellar, she determined that none of the vegetables had come from the garden. She might have known, even before descending into the murky depths. She'd already explored the surroundings and knew for a fact there wasn't a garden anywhere around the home. She'd searched and found nothing, just a few untended flowerpots and small clusters of cacti here and there.

In the spring, she'd make certain to plant a fine garden, perhaps with Annie's help. The notion pleased her. Later, as she prepared supper, Annie darted into the kitchen to get a cup of water.

"It smells good." The child eyed the pots simmering on the stove.

Caroline kneaded a batch of dough for the evening meal. "I hope you like my cooking."

Annie gave a noncommittal shrug. "Why did you sleep late?"

Caroline felt an undeniable pang of dismay. She hadn't planned to sleep in. She could see judgment clearly in the girl's eyes.

"I didn't mean to," Caroline said.

"Aunt Penny used to oversleep."

"It happens." Caroline shrugged her shoulder. "I prefer to wake early."

"You're not sick, are you?"

Caroline stopped her work. Surprise washed across her thoughts. What a peculiar question. Did she look sick? Why would Annie ask such a thing?

"I'm not ill," she replied.

"Aunt Penny used to sleep almost till lunch," Annie said, her tone forlorn.

Caroline didn't quite know what to say. She wasn't elderly, for one. Secondly, she didn't like to oversleep. And thirdly…

well, she didn't quite know how to reassure the small child or how to dismiss her curious fears.

Instead, she changed the subject to food. It was always an agreeable topic no matter what. "When I worked at the boarding house, I made a name for myself with the dinner rolls I baked each day."

Annie didn't look impressed. With a bored sigh, she set her cup on the counter.

"It probably sounds like I'm boasting," Caroline said, returning to her task. "You and Nick can be the judge."

"I reckon so."

Caroline couldn't help a flicker of irritation. The girl had criticized her rising late, which was against Caroline's nature. Then the child dismissed Caroline's cooking skills, the one thing Caroline prided herself on. In fact, Caroline had thrown herself into the task of making dinner. All day, Caroline had mulled over what to serve and how to prepare the various dishes. While it would be the first dinner of many, she wanted to impress Nick and Annie. The girl's dismissive response didn't agree with her. Not at all.

Caroline pursed her lips. "Please tell Nick I can have dinner on the table when he's ready to eat."

"Fine." Annie turned to leave.

"I'd like to ask your help."

The girl stopped in her tracks and turned to face Caroline with a frown etched on her features.

Caroline ignored her impudent glare. "Sometime before supper, I'd like you to set the table."

Annie crossed her arms. "I'm busy."

"I'll set out the plates, cups, and silverware. It won't take more than a few minutes."

"I need to help Uncle Nick."

With that, the girl marched out of the house, shutting the door with a little more force than needed. Caroline shook her head. At first, the girl's response vexed her. As the afternoon passed, she had to smile to herself. If Annie thought setting the table was a burden, she would have been quite surprised at the long list of chores Caroline had when she was a girl of nine.

It came as no surprise that Annie ignored Caroline's request. She made a point of avoiding Caroline for the rest of the day. Caroline caught a glimpse of the girl here and there. At times, she was, in fact, busy, hauling water to the corral or grooming a horse. Other times, she played and whiled away her time.

When it came time to eat, Annie skipped up the path without a care in the world. Nick followed. The fading sunlight cast a warm glow across his features. Whoever had written the letters on his behalf wasn't exaggerating. He was remarkably handsome. She had to admit it, if only to herself.

If Annie felt a shred of guilt about ignoring Caroline's request, she gave no sign. After Nick said grace, she ate with obvious approval. She had no less than four dinner rolls and two helpings of stew.

Nick didn't seem to expect much from the child. Over the course of the evening, he made remarks about her being so young and having endured so much, what with having lost her parents as well as Aunt Penny.

"This bread is delicious," Annie exclaimed, her eyes shining.

"Thank you. Perhaps you can help me make bread for tomorrow's dinner."

"No." Annie shook her head as if she didn't have a care in the world.

"No, ma'am," Nick corrected.

"No, ma'am," Annie said dutifully. "I don't know how to make bread."

"You'll learn. After all, no one's born knowing how to bake bread."

Annie laughed as if Caroline had made a fine joke. Caroline kept her expression mild and kindly. She resolved to teach the young girl how to make bread as soon as possible. The little scamp was a tad too indulged by her Uncle Nick.

"Let me help you with the dishes," Nick said as he began clearing. "It's the least I can do after you cooked the finest meal that I've eaten in I don't know how long."

"You've been working all day," Caroline argued. She reached to take the plates from his hands, but he wouldn't allow it.

"So have you."

They worked side by side, washing and drying plates.

"I've been wondering," Nick said. "Who do you suppose wrote those letters to you?"

She cringed. The entire matter left her feeling humiliated and unsure of Nick's commitment to marriage. Was he simply going through the motions for the sake of appearances? The letters had implied a marriage of convenience. Since he hadn't even written them, she couldn't imagine what the future had in store.

"I can't imagine," she said quietly. "It must be someone from Bethany Springs."

"That makes sense. But who would do such a thing? Seems mighty untoward. Sending off for a wife for a fella, without so much as a word of warning."

Caroline smiled at his teasing tone. "Warning? You make it sound ominous. Like taking a wife is akin to a terrible event, something to be avoided at all costs."

Now that she'd said the words aloud, she had to wonder if there wasn't a great deal of truth to the notion. Nick seemed perfectly content to live the life of a bachelor. And Annie had made her feelings perfectly clear. She appreciated Caroline's cooking, that was clear, but the fondness for her cooking didn't extend to Caroline herself. The girl would have been more enthusiastic if Nick had acquired a puppy in Galveston instead of a mail-order wife.

"I shouldn't have mentioned the notion of a warning. That's not what I meant." He chuckled. "I'm glad you've come, Caroline. I've received many blessings. First off, Annie. And secondly, this ranch. The McCord boys said we can live here until we're ready to live somewhere else. For me, I can't imagine living anywhere else. This place has everything we need, and it's beautiful too."

He paused before going on. When he spoke, his voice was deep, and his words slow and thoughtful. "The third blessing for me... is you."

Warmth crept over her heart. Nick couldn't imagine how much his words meant to her.

"That's kind of you," she said. "Whoever it was that wrote the letters seemed to think highly of you."

"Well, that's a nice surprise."

"I'm certain they love you and Annie a great deal."

Nick finished drying the last plate. He didn't respond and appeared deep in thought.

"Maybe it doesn't matter," Caroline added.

"I'd like to know. But it won't change a thing between us." His eyes filled with warmth. For a long moment, they shared a gaze that was almost tender.

She nodded, adding a silent prayer that she, Nick, and Annie might form a patchwork family after all. One day. Despite their inauspicious start.

Chapter Sixteen
An Unfinished Story

Caroline

At bedtime, Nick invited her to sit with him and Annie as they said evening prayers. Caroline was pleased, even if Annie seemed indifferent. Caroline went to the girl's bedroom a short while before Nick arrived. Annie sat on the side of her bed, clad in a nightgown, petting the kitten.

"Have you given him a name?" Caroline asked, taking a nearby chair.

"Yes," Annie replied shyly. "I'm calling him Pumpkin."

"That suits him. He's round and orange."

"You like kittens?"

"We weren't allowed to have pets. I've never had a cat or a dog."

"Would you like to pet him?"

Caroline smiled and went to the girl's bed. She sat on the edge and stroked the small kitten. Pumpkin might be a tiny creature, but his purr was remarkably loud. When she stopped petting him, he bumped his head against her palm.

"One day, I hope to get a dog too," Annie said. "And maybe some chickens. I'd really like to have a henhouse, with a mama hen and little chicks."

"That sounds very nice."

Caroline eyed the shelves lining the bedroom. Books filled every inch of space. "Would you like me to read you a story while we're waiting for Nick?"

Annie shrugged her shoulder, not willing to show any interest. The girl was a puzzle. One minute, she seemed friendly and almost warm. Then, she retreated into her shell.

"You certainly have a lot of books, don't you?"

Annie nodded.

"Did your Aunt Penny buy them for you? Or Nick?"

"Both. Mostly my aunt."

"Anyone can read a story aloud. Shall l tell you a story instead?"

Annie eyed her warily. "Is it a story with stepmothers?"

Caroline suppressed a smile. "It doesn't have to be."

"I don't like stepmother stories."

"You don't say. What about a story about a mother hen?"

A smile flitted across Annie's lips. "I've never heard a story about hens. I'd like that."

Caroline ran her palms across her skirts and folded her hands in her lap. "This story is about a little red hen. Such a pretty little bird. She had a baby chick which she doted on. When the chick was born, she was no more than a tiny puff of yellow fuzz. She grew quickly. Would you like to know why?"

Annie nodded; her eyes filled with interest.

"Because the little red hen was a fine cook."

The girl blinked. Another smile tugged at her lips.

"One day, the little red hen prepared a nice meal for the rest of her family, all the aunties, uncles, and cousins. She asked her little chick to help grind the flour for the cake. But do you know what that little sassy chick said to the red hen?"

Annie shook her head.

"She was too busy."

"Oh."

"The little chick hopped away to play with the baby ducklings. When little red hen asked her to mix the batter, she said she was too busy. When it was time to frost the delicious cake, the little chick refused to help with that as well."

Annie pressed her lips together with a mixture of amusement and concern.

"So later, when everyone had finished their delectable dinner, and it was time for dessert, do you know what the little red hen told her little sassy chick?"

"No."

Nick walked into the bedroom; his face wreathed in smiles. "Look at my two girls. Sitting and visiting."

Annie kept her gaze fixed on Caroline. "What did the little red hen tell the sassy chick?"

Caroline lifted her hand to cover a small, polite yawn. "Goodness, it's gotten late, hasn't it?"

Nick frowned. "I'm sure you're mighty tired. Let's pray and turn in for the night. I'm sorry I kept y'all waiting."

Chapter Seventeen
Lacking in Kindness

Nick

The next afternoon, Nick harnessed the team and took Annie and Caroline into town. He told them it was to take Caroline shopping. She'd need provisions from the mercantile. To Annie, he promised a stick of candy from the merc. In his heart, he secretly yearned to show Caroline off to the folks in Bethany Springs.

While he'd bought Caroline everything she wanted and more back in Galveston, he hadn't procured a single sack of sugar for the household. He hoped she felt secure that he could easily provide for her. As a bounty hunter, he'd earned generous compensation for his work. Most of it he'd tucked away. And when Aunt Penny passed away, she'd left a considerable inheritance as well.

He figured someday to buy his own place, but to do so now would mean he could not grow his herd. So, he thanked God for the use of Uncle Theo's ranch and prayed that someday he would be able to buy it or something similar. It didn't bother him too deeply, but the thought that he didn't own the house he slept in did gnaw at him a bit. A voice in his mind whispered to him sometimes, *A man should own his house and land.* He wasn't sure where the voice came from, but he agreed. He resolved to discuss Uncle Theo's ranch the next time he saw the McCord boys. Maybe they would consider an outright sale of the property to him. It couldn't hurt to ask.

What was most pressing was his herd - he planned to buy cattle soon. Their numbers were paltry compared to the rest of the McCord clan. He'd change that this fall. The McCord cousins liked to rib him about his ranching skill. They thought he wouldn't ever accumulate the vast herds they enjoyed. Well, as much as he loved his cousins, he was determined to show them. Old dogs could learn new tricks, even the most stubborn and ornery.

As they entered town Caroline was brimming with questions. She wanted to know about the neighboring ranches, the town of Bethany Springs, the type of people who lived there, and more.

"They're all fine folks," he assured her.

"I'm sure they are," she said, brushing aside a curl that had escaped her bonnet. A moment later, the fall breeze blew it back to her pretty face. She grumbled softly as she tried in vain to tuck it under the edge of her bonnet.

More than anything, he would have enjoyed brushing aside the mischievous, brown curl. *Was it as soft as it looked?* he wondered. But he kept his hands fixed firmly on the double reins, trying to keep his attention on the team.

"So far, everyone seems very nice. Just as I expected from your letters. Well, not your letters, but you know what I mean." She gave him a gentle smile as a teasing light lit her eyes.

He knew better than to continue that subject, what with Annie sitting right there. The last thing he wanted was to get her worked up about the letters. She'd have a lot of questions and would not hesitate to blurt out the news to folks who didn't need to know. As far as he was concerned, it was no one's business. One day, he'd find out who wrote the letters and... well, he wasn't sure what he'd do or say, but until then, he'd leave well enough alone.

Fortunately, Annie didn't seem to be listening.

"You'll like it here," he said, giving her an answering smile. "People are neighborly and try to look out for one another."

Wasn't that the truth of the matter. For the most part, anyway.

Mrs. Pittman, the mercantile owner, was on the sour side. Many times, he'd kept his opinion to himself when he talked to her, since his view of things often differed so much from hers. She was tolerable, but barely. The three of them walked up to the counter and Nick explained that Caroline was his new, mail-order bride.

"A mail-order bride!"

"That's right. We just got back from Galveston. We said our vows the very day she stepped foot in Texas."

"I'll be." Mrs. Pittman looked like she wanted to spit. She was a cantankerous, disagreeable woman. Nick almost expected her to do just that. Instead, she curled her lip as she narrowed her eyes at Caroline. Nick wished he could shield Caroline from Mrs. Pittman's venomous glare, but he needn't have worried. Caroline wasn't paying attention. Instead, his new bride examined the selection on the wall to the side of the counter.

Annie stood by Caroline's side, asking a hundred questions.

"And here I was trying to play matchmaker," Mrs. Pittman grumbled.

You and everyone else, he wanted to say, but refrained. Mrs. Pittman was the last person he'd want meddling in his affairs. Whenever the traveling preacher came round, she made a show of parading her family into services. Most of the children looked like they'd been crying. Mr. Pittman looked as henpecked a man as Nick had ever seen.

"I had all sorts of plans for you," Mrs. Pittman added.

"Thanks just the same."

She ignored his attempt to set the matter aside. "After all, you're a handsome fellow, rich, in need of a good woman to help raise that little hellion."

The force of her words took him aback.

"Mrs. Pittman, your mercantile is the nearest store for forty miles or so." He spoke quietly. "But if you ever again insult my daughter, I'll take my business the next town over, as will all my kin."

The shopkeeper reddened. She gave an indignant huff. "Well, I never!"

"Kindness doesn't cost a penny, Mrs. Pittman. Unkindness… well, that could cost a lot."

Chapter Eighteen
The Snarling Shopkeeper

Caroline

Nick seemed intent on buying out the entire mercantile. He insisted she add extra provisions to her order. When she tried to purchase a few sewing supplies, Nick began asking about, of all things, sewing machines. The shopkeeper directed him to a catalogue and, try as she might, Caroline could not persuade him to let go of the notion of buying her a sewing machine.

"I've never used a sewing machine," she told the shopkeeper, Mrs. Pittman.

The woman raised a brow. She sniffed. "Every housewife worth her salt owns a Singer."

"That might be true. But I've only recently become a housewife and I'm accustomed to sewing by hand."

"Do you at least know how to cook?"

Caroline ignored the woman's rudeness. "I suppose you'll have to ask Mr. McCord and Annie."

The woman lowered her voice. "I can't fathom why he'd send off for a mail-order wife. Not with all the young ladies vying for his attention."

Caroline's heart squeezed with a pang of dismay.

"Pretty ones too," Mrs. Pittman hissed. "Young ladies that come from fine Texas families, ladies who can cook *and* sew."

Caroline winced.

The young ladies could cook, sew and *dance*. Dancing. The one thing she didn't dare attempt. Not with her injured leg. So far, no one in Texas suspected she'd lived with a pronounced, lifelong limp. Her gait had become more even, thank goodness. The time spent walking on the ship had strengthened her legs, not to mention the work in Theo's home.

Work was a blessing, unless, in her case, it was the type of work she'd done in Boston where she'd stood all day in the boarding house kitchen, practically rooted to the spot. In her own home, the days were spent doing a blessed variety of tasks, cooking, sweeping, tidying. The variation of work suited her. Caring for a home was mending her heart, soul, and body too. Not that she'd ever share that sort of detail with such a disagreeable woman as Mrs. Pittman.

She addressed Mrs. Pittman. "I've heard of the ladies who hoped to catch my husband's eye. I'm sure they were all lovely and talented." Caroline cleared her throat and set her list on the counter. "Be that as it may, I'll need a few supplies for my sewing basket. I purchased a few things in Galveston, but still require a thimble, dressmaker's chalk, straight pins, and scissors."

Before Mrs. Pittman could summon a new batch of insults, Annie skipped across the store to Caroline's side.

"Guess what Uncle Nick wants to buy you?" she asked, her eyes shining with excitement.

"I can't imagine."

"A loom!"

"Oh, my." Caroline laughed softly.

Mrs. Pittman scoffed. "She doesn't even know how to run a sewing machine."

Caroline drew a sharp breath.

Mrs. Pittman forged ahead heedless, her tone dripping with disdain. "What's *she* going to do with a loom?"

Annie offered the shopkeeper a broad grin. "Caroline doesn't need to know how to run a sewing machine."

"You don't say," Mrs. Pittman replied.

"Or a loom," Annie added.

"How do you figure?"

Annie shrugged. "No one's *born* knowing how to use a sewing machine or a loom."

Mrs. Pittman narrowed her eyes, but before she could fuss at Annie, the girl had darted back to where Nick perused the shop catalogue.

Caroline hid a smile behind her hand. It was hard to say if Annie was being deliberately sassy or simply didn't know better. Caroline would make a point to talk to the girl about using a more respectful tone. In the meantime, she admitted a slight sense of satisfaction. Annie had spoken in her defense, whether she'd meant to or not. Caroline would take it as a small, hard-won triumph.

"Someone ought to give that girl a whooping," Mrs. Pittman declared. "If she were my daughter, she'd think twice before smarting off to her elders."

"I'm sorry, Mrs. Pittman. I'll admit Annie's manners need improving. I aim to guide her and nurture a godly spirit in the girl."

The woman snorted. "That won't happen. Not unless you can work miracles."

Clearly, the shopkeeper didn't place much faith in Caroline. Over the course of the past few days, Caroline had pondered who might have sent letters on Nick's behalf. It could have been anyone in Bethany Springs, but one thing was certain. It wasn't Mrs. Pittman. The woman seemed to regard her as a hopeless case, the same as she viewed Annie McCord.

Caroline finished making her purchases, gathered her shopping lists and prepared to leave the mercantile. As she crossed the store, the makeshift heel on her boot gave way. She stumbled. Filled with dismay, she was grateful neither Nick nor Annie saw her misstep. They were too engrossed in the shopping catalogue. She recovered her balance and continued, careful to adjust her gait.

Mrs. Pittman muttered from behind the counter. Caroline couldn't be certain but could have sworn the shopkeeper called her a clumsy invalid. When she glanced over her shoulder, Mrs. Pittman wore an expression of pure disdain.

Chapter Nineteen
A Girl from Sophie's Party

Nick

As they finished their business at the mercantile, Nick bought Annie a stick of candy. He offered to buy one for Caroline, but she shook her head, silently refusing the sweet treat. She looked pale and he wondered if she'd tired from the trip into town. She worked tirelessly each day, rising before dawn to make coffee and breakfast. After that, she cleaned and scrubbed the homestead, determined to rid the old house of every speck of dust.

As the mercantile workers loaded the wagon, Nick eyed the large purchase of provisions. Salt pork, potatoes, dried beans, cornmeal, flour. Even without the order from the butcher's shop, they had more provisions than he'd ever gotten. He wasn't concerned about the quantity, so much as the work it would entail.

"Now, Caroline, I don't want you to wear yourself out. We ought to have something simple for dinner."

A smile tugged at her lips. "I'm looking forward to making one of my best meals."

"What is it?" Annie asked.

"It's a surprise."

"I like surprises," Annie replied.

"You recall the story of the Little Red Hen?" Caroline teased.

"Yes, ma'am," Annie said without a moment's hesitation. "Especially the part about the sassy chick."

The two girls shared a laugh. A little of the color returned to Caroline's face. They chatted amiably about the contents of the shopping catalogue. Nick enjoyed thinking of buying nice things for Caroline if she'd let him. That remained to be seen.

He'd already decided one thing for certain. He wouldn't purchase any of the gifts from Mrs. Pittman. Her unkind words were a burr under his saddle pad. While he might do business with the woman as far as regular purchases went, he'd take his larger, more important business elsewhere.

She was a bitter, unpleasant woman. The less he saw of her, the better.

After the men had loaded the provisions, including the purchases from the butcher's shop, Nick helped Annie get seated on the wagon. He turned to Caroline, pleased to hold her, even for an instant as he lifted her to the wagon seat. She didn't seem inclined to enjoy his touch, but he could have sworn she drew a sharp breath when he set his hands on her narrow waist.

He was about to climb aboard when someone called his name. A young woman came down the walkway, descended the steps and approached the wagon. Her parasol shaded her face, concealing her features.

"Mr. McCord," she called. "I thought that was you!"

He squinted, still unsure who she was. Something about her voice troubled him. Her tone was overly familiar and petulant. As if she was about to fuss at him for some shortcoming. Odd, since he didn't even know who she was.

Out of habit, he took off his hat and coaxed a smile to his lips. "Hello."

"You don't remember me, do you?"

"Well, let's see." He racked his mind for the name of the young lady. He didn't want to offend. On the other hand, he had to admit he didn't recall who she was. His skin prickled with discomfort, aware of Caroline and Annie sitting on the wagon, just a pace or two behind him.

"It's Juliet Williams. From the party at Sophie McCord's home."

As she approached, she tilted her parasol, and the movement allowed him to see her face better. She looked vaguely familiar. Had they danced? Darn. If only he'd remembered a few of the ladies from that day. He didn't, however. Maybe because he was trying to forget.

"Miss Williams," he stammered.

A few vague memories flitted across his thoughts. The Williams clan was a wealthy cattle ranching family from the valley. They had one large property near Edinburg and another near Laredo. He seemed to recall Aunt Sophie saying that Juliet was the only child and the apple of her father's eye. The day of the garden party, Aunt Sophie had practically begged him to court the girl. Then again, she'd begged him to court any girl, not just Juliet Williams.

He tugged at his suddenly too-tight collar. "Nice to see you again."

Heavens, he was a terrible liar.

Miss Williams laughed and waved her gloved hand. "I'd hoped to hear from you one day. Especially since we never got a chance to two-step. I keep hearing about how well you dance."

"You do?" he asked.

She batted her lashes. "Your dancing skills are the stuff of legends."

Annie snorted behind him.

Nick winced at Miss William's remark and obvious flirtation. If only he could get her to be on her way or at least stop talking about that unpleasant afternoon at Sophie's party. While Nick hadn't done anything wrong or untoward, he didn't care for the notion of Caroline hearing Miss Williams carry on.

"Did you happen to hear anything else?" He turned to the wagon and held out his arm. "I've recently gotten married. Allow me to introduce my wife, Caroline. Caroline, this is Juliet Williams."

Miss Williams's gasp was followed by a deep frown. She glared at Caroline, making no attempt to disguise her disapproval.

"Pleased to meet you," Caroline said politely.

"Uh-huh," Miss Williams said, gawking at Caroline, still too stunned to say much more.

"She's a good cook," Annie chimed in. The girl wore a mischievous grin as if she knew perfectly well that Nick was squirming with discomfort.

"Is she the little orphan girl?" Miss Williams asked, wrinkling her nose.

Nick gritted his teeth. "No. Annie's my daughter."

"Uh-huh."

Annie eyed Miss Williams as if she was considering a smart reply. Caroline set her hand on the girl's shoulder and said something Nick couldn't hear. Annie shrugged and went back to enjoying her stick of candy, ignoring Miss Williams.

"We'd best be on our way," Nick replied. "If you'll excuse us."

Miss Williams set her hand on his arm and spoke, her voice lowered. "Who is she? I didn't see her at the party. Where is she from?"

"She's not from around these parts," Nick replied, not willing to say more. He was fairly certain Miss Williams wouldn't have anything nice to say about him settling down with a mail-order bride.

"Nice to see you again, Miss Williams," he said, stepping away, his tone firm to make clear that the conversation was over. He put on his Stetson, nodded a silent goodbye, and climbed to his seat. From the corner of his eye, he glimpsed her standing stock-still, staring after them with disbelief.

They pulled away from the mercantile. Nick didn't bother with a backward glance but could practically feel the girl's gaze boring into his shoulders.

Chapter Twenty
The Man is the Frame,
The Lady is the Picture

Caroline

After they returned from town, the overcast sky darkened, and it began to drizzle. Most days, Nick rode out into the pastures to inspect fences or check on his cattle. He had a few dozen head of cattle, and he made sure to get his eyes on each one of them every day he could. Perhaps it was because he was just starting out, but he liked to see with his own eyes that they were doing all right. Today's rain prevented him from checking the livestock.

Instead, he worked in the barn. Caroline picked her way down the path, careful not to slip on the slick trail. Her leg seemed stronger each day. Still, she hoped the drizzle wouldn't turn into a deluge.

The tall double doors stood open. She stepped inside and wiped the raindrops from her face with a small lace hanky. She'd explored the house and surroundings, but this was the first time she'd come to the barn, and it was larger than she expected. An aisle ran the length. Stalls bordered the sides. Horses moved around their enclosures, chewing hay, and stamping their hooves. A soft whinny drifted across the quiet of the barn as the rain began to come down more heavily.

She searched the various rooms for feed and saddles and found Nick in a small workshop tucked beneath a corner hayloft. She stopped in the doorway and watched him as he bent over a saddle. He didn't notice her. Instead, he fixed his attention on his work, a small saddle perched on a wooden mount. He tapped a nail into the leather.

His brow was knit with concentration. His hair was rumpled, probably because when he grew frustrated, he liked to rake his fingers through the chestnut waves. His jaw was shadowed with the growth of a two-day old beard. He often forgot to shave and would cheerfully apologize for his rough appearance, citing his years as a solitary bounty hunter. He pressed his mouth to a thin line to hold several nails tightly between his lips.

Nick McCord was remarkably handsome. She had to admit it, if only to herself. And yet, why bother denying the fact? Juliet McCullough had certainly noticed and seemed to have set her sights on him some time ago. Why, Caroline wondered, hadn't Nick chosen the lovely, obviously wealthy, society girl over a penniless mail-order bride? One who had arrived in Texas, shipwrecked on a desolate coastline. Oh, and he hadn't even invited her either. She just showed up.

He could have sent Caroline on her way. Instead, he'd agreed to the marriage. She was grateful. She desperately hoped he wouldn't regret his decision.

She cleared her throat. "Hello, Nick."

He lifted his head up in surprise. Instead of responding, he gazed at her and smiled, dropping one of the nails from his lips. Chuckling, he bent down to retrieve it. He straightened and set the hammer and nails aside.

"Caroline. You never venture down to the barn."

"I was looking for you." Warmth heated her face. How ridiculous she must sound. They were so rarely alone. Most of the time, Annie was nearby, providing a welcome distraction.

"You need help?" Nick frowned. "I talked to Annie about minding you and doing as you asked. Don't want you to wear yourself out."

Despite her awkward discomfort, she smiled inwardly. Nick seemed to think she was fragile. That she'd find her tasks too much to manage when, in fact, tending their household filled her with happiness. She enjoyed cleaning and tidying the large ranch house. And she especially loved cooking. Making a home for the three of them gave her more contentment than she'd ever known.

She had much to be grateful for. She did her best not to think of all the lovely girls who had vied for Nick's attention. She'd come to Texas to care for Annie. That was the most important matter. Nick's past romantic inclinations were something she didn't want to think about.

"Annie's helping. I left her with some linens to fold." After Caroline had told the story of the Little Red Hen, Annie had been more willing to lend a hand. Perhaps not eager, but at least the girl complied with Caroline's requests. It was progress.

He crossed the workroom, stopping a few paces away and folding his arms across his chest. "Is it time for supper already?"

"No." She shook her head. Her heart thudded inside her chest. She summoned her courage and held out one of her boots. It belonged to one of the pairs he'd bought her in Galveston. "I'd like to ask for your assistance. With my boot."

He stared at the boot. "All right."

Slowly, he reached for the boot, giving her a bewildered look.

Part of her was pleased she'd managed to disguise her limp so well that he didn't know of her troubles. On the other hand, she wished she didn't need to tell him anything, but there was no way around it. She needed his help with her boot, and she needed to tell him why. She'd rather have him think of her as perfectly lovely and without any blemish, but that was fairy-tale thinking. It was time to tell him.

She offered the ragged scrap she'd loosened in the mercantile earlier that day. "I made this patch out of the material we purchased in Galveston. I need a little extra height on one boot heel."

"You do?"

She swallowed hard. "Yes, well, otherwise, I tend to trip."

He took the scrap. "I see. I hadn't noticed."

He hadn't noticed? Caroline wouldn't allow herself to believe that. He was merely being polite, nothing more.

"I tried to alter the boots on my own, but I don't have what I need. Especially since I've lost so many of my belongings."

She cringed inwardly. The last thing she wanted was to sound pitiful or to draw attention to her unfavorable circumstances. She didn't want pity. Or judgment. Mrs. Pittman had called her a clumsy invalid. What if Nick viewed her as a clumsy invalid? She'd die a little inside if her husband ever showed a modicum of pity.

Worse, what if he viewed her injury in the same way as the caretakers at the orphanage? She didn't remember the accident. All she knew was that she'd fallen down the stairs as a toddler. The doctors expected a full recovery. When that didn't happen, her caretakers implied she'd somehow failed. What had lingered since her early childhood was the notion that she had disappointed everyone, and that she was broken, somehow.

To her dismay, Nick grumbled with irritation. Turning away, he crossed the workshop and returned to his bench. Setting the saddle aside, he groused under his breath.

"Is there something the matter?" she asked. Perhaps she shouldn't have come to the barn to ask for help. It might have been better to manage the matter on her own just as she had done for as long as she could remember.

Thunder rumbled in the distance. The rain fell steadily, drumming on the barn roof.

"Is this the reason why you don't want to dance with me?" He held up the boot.

Caroline blinked with confusion. The last thing she expected was for him to broach the subject of *dancing*. Not when she'd practically bared her soul to him. Or that's what it felt like, judging by the raw feeling inside.

"I don't know how to dance," she said, lifting her chin. She wanted to throw in a comment about Juliet Williams but didn't want to sound petulant or childish.

"So what?"

"Well..." Her words died away as she tried to summon a proper argument.

"No one's born knowing how to dance."

She gave a breathless laugh at hearing her own words spoken by Nick.

He studied the cotton patch she'd fashioned for her boot, turning it over a time or two before tossing it aside. Caroline stared with disbelief as it flew through the air and landed on top of a pile of debris in the corner. Her hand-stitched patch was hardly something for the debris pile. She was about to protest. That patch had cost her several hours of work, stitching by lamplight, only to be discarded like so much rubbish.

Shocked and more than a little indignant, she watched him intently. He seemed entirely unconcerned. No. Instead of troubling himself about her discarded handiwork, he selected a scrap of leather from a nearby basket, picked up a pair of shears and began trimming the scrap into a small, heel-shaped patch. "I can show you how to dance," Nick said in a casual tone.

"But. Well..." What to say to his invitation? She'd summoned her courage to speak to him about her boot. After she revealed her troubles, the conversation had somehow turned to the subject of them dancing. "Er," she added for no good reason, cringing inwardly at her foolish response.

"It's not difficult." He lifted his gaze to meet hers. A smile tugged at his lips. "Especially for the lady."

"Not difficult?"

He turned her shoe over, so the heel faced up and braced it between two heavy blocks of wood. "Right."

"You say it's not difficult for the lady. Are you suggesting it's a terrible chore for the gentleman? Especially one so renowned for his dancing skill."

There. She'd said it. She'd given in to her childish impulses. She thought she was above such foolishness, but her consternation around Nick's past bubbled up from her inner most thoughts and flowed out of her mouth before her reasonable self could stop it. She wasn't ashamed, however. If anything, she felt a small thrill of victory.

Nick wasn't bothered by her remark. Far from it. A smile tugged at his lips. Instead of replying, he began hammering the leather patch, affixing it to the sole of her boot. The nails were short, just a fraction of an inch and it only took him two gentle taps to drive each nail into the sole. In no time at all, he'd completed the task.

He tried to twist the leather patch free. When it refused to budge, he returned it to her, along with an infuriating grin. "Dancing with you, Mrs. McCord, wouldn't be a chore. Not at all."

"Show-off." Caroline couldn't disguise the petulance in her tone. She snatched the boot from his hand, deliberately avoiding his gaze.

"I do want to show off." He took her wrist in his hand, clasping it gently since she held her boot firmly. He set his other hand gently upon her waist. "I'd like to hold you in my arms and show off my pretty wife."

"Please, Nick." Wincing with mortification, she could hardly meet his gaze.

"Nothing wrong with a man dancing with his bride," Nick said gently. "And you should know something. Dancing isn't a chance for a fella to show off."

Caroline kept her eyes averted, wishing more than anything to escape. "Fine."

"It's for a fella to show off his girl."

This gave her pause. She wasn't familiar with the intricacies of courting, much less dancing. Part of her wondered how on earth he knew. She spoke shyly. "I'd never heard that before."

"It's true."

"Thank you for explaining." She wanted to put an end to the discussion.

Nick, however, had more to say. He crossed his arms and leaned against a saddle rack. Caroline could tell he hoped to discuss this at length. "The important thing to remember about dancing is that it goes far deeper than just sliding your boots around some dusty floor."

Caroline pressed her lips together.

"First of all, the lady's giving her trust to the fellow, which is a lovely notion if you think about it. He's taking her in his arms, and they move as one. And if the fellow knows what he's doing, everyone notices the lady, not the man."

"That's a lovely sentiment. I should get back to the-"

"If a fellow knows what he's doing when he takes a lady in his arms, he's nothing more than a frame."

She lifted her gaze to meet his. "I don't quite follow."

Nick's voice softened. "If a fellow knows what he's doing, he's no more than the frame." A warmth lit his eyes. "And his lady is the picture."

His words sounded so kind and so caring she hardly knew what to say. All along, she'd considered him decent and upstanding, to be sure, but rarely did he seem tender. Perhaps he was tender with Annie, especially at night when they prayed together, but the rest of the time he was more matter of fact.

Her breath caught fast in her throat, snaring her reply. She could hardly draw breath, much less dare to believe his words.

Nick stroked a thumb across her cheek to brush away a lock of hair. "God put us together for a reason. I have faith in the Lord's providence."

She nodded slowly, wishing she could summon a response.

He continued. "And one day, when you finally agree to dance with me, I'll be showing off my sweet bride."

"Nick." She stepped away to gain a little distance from his endearing words. "I'm not sure I'm an adequate dance partner."

"I disagree." With a playful smile, he lifted his hands, holding one at shoulder level, the other near his mid-section, mimicking a dance posture. He took a few quick steps, surprisingly graceful for a man of his height. "You're not an *adequate* dance partner, you're *my* dance partner, till death do us part."

She shook her head.

"Together, we'll be more than adequate."

"I believe it." His playful smile faded. "God brought you here for a reason. I don't know who wrote you those letters, but I believe your coming is a blessing."

Her eyes stung with the threat of tears.

He went on. "Ever since my aunt asked me to care for Annie, I've received more blessings than I can count. Annie was the first. Next came this house and ranch. Then I got a few dozen cattle at a bargain price. Then you arrived. I didn't ask for a bit of that, but God blessed me anyway."

He grimaced. "Not to compare you to a bunch of bargain cattle. But you know what I mean. I hope. Land sakes."

She smiled.

"This wooing business is a sight harder than I ever expected," he said with an awkward chuckle.

A lump formed in her throat. The tenderness in his voice unraveled a small knot around her heart. She felt equally blessed. His mention of Annie, as a blessing rather than as a burden, tugged at her heart. As much as she preferred to keep matters of her heart neatly bound, tucked away, safe and secure, Nick seemed determined to find it and embrace it, regardless.

Chapter Twenty-One
Hearts and Swirls

Caroline

That evening, just before Caroline finished dinner, she realized she needed apples from the root cellar. Annie played quietly in her room. Caroline ventured down the hallway and stopped in the doorway. She was about to ask Annie to help her, but she paused for a moment. The sight of the girl brought a smile to her lips.

Annie lay on her bed, drawing pictures, the kitten curled up beside her. Annie was so absorbed in her task that she didn't notice Caroline standing there. She doodled on a pad of paper. Colored pencils lay scattered across the bed.

Caroline knocked gently on the doorframe. Annie looked up and blinked with bewilderment. She'd been so lost in her artwork, she'd forgotten everything, or so it seemed. Caroline found the notion endearing. She recalled such moments when she was a child, especially when she played music or listened to others play.

A sweet smile curved the girl's lips. "Mama Hen," she said with a giggle.

Caroline had to laugh. Annie had certainly taken the tale of the red hen to heart. Caroline returned the joking sentiment, calling the child, "Sassy Chick."

They shared a laugh.

Outside, it was still dark and drizzling, but the inside of the ranch house felt warm and inviting, especially after sharing a heart-warming exchange with Annie.

"Is it dinnertime?" Annie asked, knitting her brow. "Already?"

"Almost." Caroline wandered into the room. "May I see what you're drawing?"

"Nothing special. Just a pony. Right now, I have to take old Jesper when Uncle Nick lets me ride. I'd really like my own pony. Not an old ornery, sway-backed fellow like Jesper."

Caroline drew closer and eyed the girl's drawing. Annie had drawn a picture of a chestnut pony with a blaze and four white socks. It appeared to prance amid a meadow filled with daisies. With a smile, Caroline noticed the addition of ducks, puppies, and several lambs. Annie didn't disguise her love of animals or her desire to acquire as many as possible.

As Caroline studied the picture, she got a peculiar feeling. It was as if she'd seen it before. But that wasn't possible. She frowned and looked closer. Why did it seem familiar? Her gaze drifted to the border of the page. Annie had drawn a frame around her pony picture. Not a solid frame, but one lined with hearts and delicate, little swirls.

Slowly, it dawned on her. She'd seen those very hearts and swirls on the letters she'd received from Nick. Or, better said, the letters she thought had come from Nick.

Caroline traced her finger along the decorative edge. She whispered, "That's very pretty."

"Thank you."

"So delicate. And feminine."

"My friend Elsie showed me how to make a pretty border on my pictures. That's what she always does and now I do too."

"Elsie?" Caroline recalled hearing of the child, but now wasn't certain who she was related to. There were many Honeycutts and McCords. It was difficult to keep everyone straight in her mind, to remember who belonged to whom. Especially since she could no longer refer to any of the original letters.

"She's Molly and Daniel's adopted daughter. Do you want to draw with me?" Annie asked.

The child's innocent question jarred Caroline from her surprise and confusion. She looked up at Caroline with a happy, expectant expression.

"No. No thank you."

A flicker of disappointment passed behind the child's eyes. Instantly, Caroline regretted her response. It wasn't often that Annie sought her out. Never, if Caroline was honest with herself.

"Okay," Annie returned to her task and proceeded to ignore her.

"I need something from the root cellar. Apples."

Annie didn't reply. Instead, she picked up a green pencil and began coloring the grass beneath the pony's hooves.

Caroline tried again. "Would you fetch me a half-dozen apples? Please."

The girl didn't reply immediately. Silence stretched between them. A moment before, Caroline's thoughts spun around the notion of the decorative hearts and who might have drawn them. When Annie ignored her request, Caroline's mind switched to a more immediate issue, that of Annie's willfulness. Was it because Caroline had refused the child's invitation to draw?

Heavens, children could be trying. She sighed, a sense of defeat creeping over her.

Annie spoke quietly. "I'm afraid of the root cellar."

"Afraid?" Caroline's thoughts took yet another sharp turn. She hadn't expected that sort of reply from Annie. The child was afraid. Caroline had assumed Annie was merely being obstinate, as usual.

"Yes, ma'am." She glanced over her shoulder, her expression filled with uneasiness. "It's dark down there."

Caroline nodded. "All right."

It was clear that Annie was being sincere. The last thing she wanted was to frighten the small child. Quite the opposite. Caroline yearned to forge a bond with the girl.

Annie spoke in a tremulous tone. "And the door closes on its own."

"I see." Caroline turned to leave. "I didn't realize."

Annie continued. "You have to be careful."

"Right."

"You must prop it open. There's a big rock to the side of the door." Annie set her pencil aside. "I'll show you."

Caroline nodded. "Thank you."

She smiled inwardly. When she decided to come to Texas, she yearned for a sense of belonging, not just a warmer climate that would be more agreeable to her injured leg. She'd never imagined how a family might tug her emotions every which way. It was unpredictable. Not just in terms of the child, Annie, but her husband too. One thing was certain; her heart hadn't been prepared for any of this.

They went out the kitchen door, around to the root cellar. The doors were shut with a board shoved through the handles. When Caroline had explored the cellar a few days prior, the doors had been open. She soon found it was no easy task to wrench them open. Annie lent a hand, pulling with all her might. After a few attempts, they managed to pry them open and wedge a rock beneath.

Annie grinned. "We did it, Mama Hen."

Caroline brushed aside a stray curl that had escaped her careful arrangement. She grinned at Annie. "We did, Sassy Chick. Indeed, we did. Thank you."

Chapter Twenty-Two
The Girls Gang Up

Nick

When his work was done and it was time to head home, Nick fed the animals and closed the barn. He hurried up the path, eager to escape the steady downpour. Raindrops stung his face. His shirt was soon soaked.

Light glowed from the windows of the ranch house. The welcoming sight filled his heart with warmth. The savory aroma, which was almost as welcoming, hit him a dozen paces from the house. Even though he already knew Caroline was a fine cook, the scent was even better than he expected. By the time he took a few more steps, his stomach was rumbling.

A smile tugged at his lips. He was grateful. For several reasons, but especially for the simple reason he and Annie weren't going to suffer through another pan of scrambled eggs and stale biscuits for dinner. There was more to that agreeable prospect. He'd enjoy a fine meal at the end of the day, and he'd do so in the company of his beautiful wife.

The bride he never expected.

He took the porch steps two at a time, a sweet thrill of expectation crossing his thoughts. Caroline. She waited inside Theo's house. How was it possible his surprise bride had made a house a home?

An hour earlier, he'd tried his best to charm her in the barn, failing miserably. The suggestion of gathering her in his arms and dancing hadn't been agreeable to his tenderhearted bride, what with her notions of an old troublesome leg injury. She exaggerated. He was certain. She was perfectly fine.

He'd dance with her. One day.

Crossing the porch, a new thought came to mind. Caroline didn't want to rush things. She conjured all manner of excuses, all in the interest of taking her time when it came to the delicate matters of marriage. She was shy. He'd need to respect that.

He stepped inside, closing the door behind him as he pulled off his boots. He called a greeting before heading to his room to change his wet shirt.

Laughter drifted from the kitchen. Annie and Caroline joked. Something about mother hens and baby chicks. Nick couldn't imagine the topic of their conversation. Menfolk had ways of talking that were privy only to other men, subjects they kept to themselves, notions that lay outside female understanding. He supposed women were the same. They shared things with each other, notions they'd never speak of to any man.

Their laughter pleased him. It warmed his heart. Suddenly, he realized this was exactly what he hoped for ever since he'd set eyes on Annie. Perhaps even before. That he'd take a wife who would care for Annie and love her.

"You're wrong," Caroline stated. "Nick's not that way."

"No, ma'am." Annie giggled. "I know my Uncle Nick. I'm certain that I'm right."

"That *is* surprising. I would never have guessed."

"You'll see, Mama Hen."

"I believe you're wrong, Sassy Chick."

He knit his brow. On the one hand, Annie was minding her manners with Caroline. He'd prefer that she use 'ma'am' instead of 'Mama Hen' but the term of endearment showed progress.

On the other hand, he'd like to know what the heck they were talking about. What did Annie need to explain to Caroline? Land sakes. He liked to think his manners were respectable enough. What if Annie revealed something he'd like to keep hidden? Some bad habits, for example, maybe something left over from his bounty hunter days.

"He does it all the time," Annie said.

The child's authoritative tone struck an unexpected nerve. What were they discussing exactly?

Caroline laughed softly. "Really?"

No. He answered silently, only to himself. He wasn't one to do regular, predictable sorts of things. The sound of the oven door closing combined with water pouring into a wash basin.

What he'd very much like to know was, what was it that he did all the time? Some random thing Annie had noticed. Without a moment's hesitation, he silently dismissed her observation. He didn't do anything predictable. He was Nick McCord. Sly. Stealthy. He was a renowned bounty hunter, one hired for big pay, not one that had expected mannerisms. Certainly not anything a nine-year-old girl might notice.

Annie had to be wrong.

"The way he gestures when he wants to make a point," Caroline said.

He gestured?

A brief silence hung in the air. In the quiet interim, Nick imagined Caroline mimicking his so-called gestures. A moment later, both Caroline and Annie burst into laughter.

What now? He didn't gesture. He held out his hands and stared at them as he pondered the notion. Did he gesture?

"Like the time he was talking about the fence along the back pasture," Annie said.

"Or the only way to correctly crank the water pump," Caroline suggested.

More laughter.

He shook his head as he crossed the sitting room, a smile tugging at his lips. Another burst of laughter drifted from the kitchen. The women in his home had gone from adversaries to allies in the blink of an eye, leaving him the odd man out. The two of them conspired. So be it. At least they were making what smelled like a mighty appetizing dinner. Some sort of roast and perhaps a savory potato dish. His mouth watered.

He resolved to ignore the girls' antics as he sorted through his mail. Annie left the kitchen and gave a cry of surprise when she found him sitting at his desk. She drew close to his side and wrapped her arm around his neck.

"You being a good girl, Little Bit?"

"I'm being helpful," she said quietly with a note of pride. "And polite."

He smiled as he opened the various envelopes and studied their contents. "I appreciate that. Very much. Dinner smells good."

"I made the rolls. Caroline showed me how this morning right after breakfast. She taught me how to start the yeast, add the flour, let it rest, punch it down and let it rest again. It takes a long time."

"You don't say."

"We started making dinner rolls an hour after breakfast."

"I can't wait to try one," he murmured as he opened the last letter in the pile.

"Caroline thinks you'll eat at least three rolls. We made a wager."

"Did you now?"

"If I'm wrong, she says she'll make sweet rolls on Sunday before we go to hear the traveling preacher in Bethany Springs."

"Three? What if I eat more?" Annie replied but he didn't pay much mind. Instead, he read the final letter and noted a swell of satisfaction. "I just got word. There's a herd of two hundred head of crossbreeds in Comal County."

Annie dropped her arm and eyed him warily. "What does that mean?"

"Well, I'm going to fetch them. Bring them home."

"Can I come with you?"

He shook his head. "No. Of course not. You'll stay here with Caroline."

The girl paled. He wondered why she'd find that objectionable. Caroline was kind as the day was long. She and Annie got along well, judging by their joking banter. Why would Annie find the notion troubling? Part of him wanted to point out that the reason he'd exchanged vows was on her behalf. But in the back of his mind, he had to admit, that wasn't the truth. Not entirely.

"Caroline?" Annie asked quietly.

"That's right."

"My stepmother?"

Nick grumbled under his breath. "Hush now. Don't carry on about stepmothers. Are there any stories of wicked stepdaughters?"

Annie didn't like his joke and looked affronted.

Heavens. The girl's sad eyes could undo him in a heartbeat. When she looked at him with that melancholy expression, she'd wreck his every intention. He'd set out trying to be stern or maybe even a little severe. Then Annie would give him that look, and all his intentions would melt like dew on a warm morning.

He set his hand over hers and kissed her forehead. "Don't fret, Little Bit. I won't be gone for long. And when I return, I'll come back with more cattle than we can shake a stick at."

Annie didn't look convinced.

He went on. "Over the winter, they'll fatten up. In the spring, I'll send them off to market and buy you a pony."

Why he'd promised a pony, he couldn't say. She was forever begging for more animals. If she had her way, they'd have their own zoo. Annie's expression of delight made him determined to fulfill his promise. He'd do anything for Annie. Or Caroline. His two girls each had him wrapped around their little finger. He was outnumbered. But he wasn't complaining. Not a bit.

Chapter Twenty-Three
Trapped

Caroline

Dawn broke late on the morning Nick was to leave the ranch to buy cattle. The skies were dark and threatening. Caroline saw him off, with a satchel of food for his travels. Annie stood by her side. The girl hardly spoke at first. She'd campaigned valiantly for the chance to accompany Nick. He'd argued that the long ride was too much for the small girl. She was offended. More than offended. She was *wounded*. Especially since not accompanying him on the trip meant staying with the dreaded stepmother.

"We'll be fine," Caroline assured him as he mounted his horse.

"Probably not," Annie added.

"And why is that?" Nick asked, his tone edged with humor.

"Because I have to stay here... alone." Annie's resentment was palpable.

The drizzle dampened not just the three of them but their mood as well. Nick's horse pawed the dirt. Rain dripped off Nick's hat and dampened his clothing. Off in the distance, thunder rumbled. Caroline felt a peculiar longing in her heart. She didn't want Nick to leave, even though she knew he set off to do exactly what he needed to do to become a cattleman. She hated to see him set off to parts unknown.

Nick put on a pair of gloves and adjusted his Stetson. "You won't be alone, Little Bit. Caroline will be here."

Caroline had wanted to point out the same. She was grateful Nick had said it first. His words lent some credence to the idea.

Annie snorted, as if she thought staying with Caroline was every bit as terrible as staying alone.

Caroline didn't want Nick to worry about anything while he was gone. After all, this was why she'd come to Texas, to tend to Annie. It was only since she'd arrived in Texas and learned the truth about the letters that other notions had come to the forefront. Like dancing and matrimony. Holding hands. All those uncomfortable subjects.

She spoke, trying her best to sound cheerful. "We'll be fine, Nick. I'll take care of everything while you're gone."

He nodded, keeping his eyes fixed on hers.

"And when you return," she added, "we'll celebrate."

His brows lifted. She flushed.

"Somehow," she added. "Perhaps a picnic out in the pastures, to see the new cattle."

"That sounds mighty fine," he replied, his expression inscrutable.

"Mostly, I don't want you to worry," she added, gesturing awkwardly. "About anything here. On the ranch. Or Annie."

"Oh, don't you worry," Annie said, her tone bitter. "I'll be fine. Probably. Maybe."

Nick chuckled. "You'll be more than fine, I'm certain. I wouldn't head out if I thought otherwise." He bid them goodbye and turned his horse to set off into the gray drizzle. Despite the downpour, both Annie and Caroline stood rooted to the spot, watching him until he was no more than a speck on the horizon.

When they could no longer see him, they trudged back to the house. Their boots sloshed in the mud. Pumpkin waited for them at the top of the steps, mewing piteously. The kitten had the good sense to stay out of the rain. Annie scooped her up and headed inside.

Caroline resisted the urge to follow. She'd let the girl pout for a time. If need be, Caroline would remind her of the story of the Little Red Hen. It seemed a good comparison to the child's general reluctance. At the same time, she knew these sorts of things took time, like untangling a pile of yarn. It took time and patience. She resolved to keep working at it, until it was completely unraveled.

Caroline ignored Annie's recalcitrance. She had to trust that in time the girl would come around. Instead, she focused on what she did best. She swept the upstairs rooms. When the rain cleared and the sun began to shine, she dragged the carpets outside. She beat them with a broom and hung them over the low-hanging limbs of the surrounding oak trees.

She was vaguely aware of Annie. At times, the girl ventured outside. Other times, she tended to her kitten and played indoors. To the girl's credit, she also did as Nick had asked and tended to the animals in the barn. Nick had taken his best horse, which left a fair number of horses and animals that required care. Fortunately, Annie knew what to do.

Caroline offered to help but her offer was met with a silent, resentful shrug.

Caroline made a point of ignoring the girl's rude behavior. She was determined to let the child be. Annie would come around in time. Of that, Caroline was certain. As a young girl, Caroline had seen it happen time and again when new children had arrived at the front step of the orphanage.

The children appeared, clutching their small satchels, looking frightened and utterly alone in the world, unless of course, they arrived with an equally frightened sibling. It took time for the new children to overcome their past, heal their shattered hearts, and to trust others.

Annie wasn't as downtrodden as the children Caroline remembered, but she had many of the same characteristics. Her eyes held small glimmers of fear. She fretted unnecessarily for reasons that made no sense. Other times, the girl found happiness in the smallest gesture.

After Caroline tended to the cleaning upstairs, she set about preparing a good dinner for her and Annie. With Nick gone, she nevertheless intended to serve a savory meal, even if the child refused to acknowledge her efforts.

It would be a fine meal if she did say so herself. She'd make fried chicken, cabbage slaw, mashed potatoes, and gravy. She might even bake an apple cake.

As much as she resented Annie's willful ways, Caroline couldn't help feeling sorry for the child. Each time Caroline caught a glimpse of the child throughout the day, Annie looked downright mournful. Poor little thing. Annie clearly felt Nick's absence keenly, even more so than Caroline.

Caroline did feel a bit lost without Nick around. Since she'd come to live in Theo's home, he was always somewhere nearby. Often, he worked in the barn or in the fields checking the cattle, and other times, closer to the house, like when he mended the roof or split wood for the fireplace.

In the late afternoon, a cool wind blew from the north. It struck Caroline as a surprise. While she was no stranger to cold weather, the temperatures had been temperate. Not once had she donned a shawl or coat. But the northern winds brought a cold climate she hadn't expected, or at least not so soon. From what she'd heard, cold weather wasn't due until the end of September, not the first weeks of the month.

She hauled wood inside, trying not to fret about Nick. Had he packed warm clothes? Did he ride through rain and stormy weather? Heavens, if only he were nearby, she'd let him hold her hand and even draw her into some clumsy excuse for a dance. If only he were near.

After a fair bit of struggle, she started a fire in the hearth. It seemed meager, a poor excuse for a fire, but it was done. She eyed the weak flames with dismay. By the time she returned to the kitchen, the bread was scorched.

She muttered under her breath with disappointment. More than anything, she'd dearly hoped to sit down with Annie and share a lovely meal, just the two of them together.

She realized one thing was lacking for the meal, cinnamon for the cake. Most of the spices were stored in the root cellar. She was about to call Annie but decided to wait until she was ready to put the finishing touches on the cake.

She stepped outside the kitchen and hauled open the door of the root cellar. As she lifted the heavy door, a gust of wind blew. The strong wind pinned the door down. Caroline tried again. The door refused to budge. On the third attempt, she managed to pull the door open. With immense effort, she swung it aside. She didn't bother trying to open the other door. She hurried down the shadowed stairwell and peered into the dim corners. Where was the rack of spices exactly?

As she tried to recall the contents of the cellar, a brisk wind blew overhead. It was no more than a single gust of wind, less than the brutal winter winds she'd encountered in Boston. And yet, it was enough to blow the door shut. The slam of the door shook the steps. In an instant, she was trapped in the dark depths of the cellar.

Chapter Twenty-Four
Cattle and Gifts in Comal County

Nick

The morning's travel went better than expected despite the steady rainfall. Ever since Nick had moved into Theo's homestead, he'd worked hard to start and grow a respectable herd. After all, he was a McCord, and every McCord he knew worked hard.

He hadn't grown up ranching, not like his cousins. His father was a lawman like him. He grew up in a small town outside San Antonio. All he'd ever wanted was to do the same type of work his father did, even after his father died tracking down a minor outlaw.

Despite losing his father when he was scarcely more than a boy, not to mention the passing of his mother a few years later, all he ever wanted to do was be like his daddy, a lawman of the highest caliber. His father was driven by a need to protect others from the criminal element. Nick was inspired by the very same goal.

For the most part, he found his work meaningful and liked to think that his father would have approved. His mother, he knew, would most definitely not have approved. Come to think of it, she and Aunt Penny were probably of a like mind on the subject.

Everything changed when he got the letter informing him of Aunt Penny's passing away. Now, all he wanted was to provide a good home for his family.

There was still a fair bit of ambition stirring in his heart. His cousins were prosperous. They'd encouraged him in his efforts, offering advice and support. They wanted to see him succeed as well. He'd written a letter to Paul, thanking him again for use of Theo's ranch, but also asking if he could buy the ranch outright. He wasn't sure when he'd have the money to do that, but he wanted to at least start the conversation, so that Paul and his brothers would know about Nick's ambitions.

As the day wore on and he traveled further and further from the ranch, his eagerness gave way to other notions. His thoughts returned again and again to Caroline and Annie. How were they faring? Were they managing? Was Annie on her best behavior as he'd instructed? Another thought lingered in the back of his mind. One he'd never want to admit to anyone. Did Caroline miss him anywhere as much as he missed her?

He certainly liked to think so.

Late in the afternoon on the second day, when he arrived at the Comal County stockyard, he completed his business in less than a couple of hours' time. After some small bit of haggling, he managed to purchase close to 100 head of Longhorn-Angus mixed breeds. The rancher even offered to have his men deliver the herd to Bethany Springs.

He concluded his business with a simple handshake and found he still had some daylight left to explore the local mercantile. The store owner was a great deal more pleasant than Mrs. Pittman. Then again, that might be true of every other store owner in the state of Texas.

Mr. Henne was an older man, probably in his sixties. He carried two sets of eyeglasses, *one to see the tip of his nose and one to see the tip of yours*, he said more than once. He had recently received a new delivery of a Singer sewing machine and a loom, and he was excited to show Nick how they worked.

Nick needed little convincing. After five minutes he purchased them both. The notion of presenting Caroline with not one but two gifts pleased him more than he could say. Not forgetting about Annie, he made sure to purchase a gift for her too, several fairy tales he'd heard about but had never seen in Bethany Springs. The shopkeeper offered to deliver the goods in a week's time. Nick left the store the happiest man in Comal County, heck, maybe the happiest man in Texas.

The rain fell steadily. Despite the gloomy weather, Nick resolved to start his return to Bethany Springs that day instead of spending the night in town. He'd ride until he couldn't stay awake, or until he couldn't see the path. He was certain he could traverse the difficult terrain. He had faith in his tracking skills as well as the good horse sense of his trusty gelding.

But he'd not counted on the weather getting worse. By 10pm the light rain had turned into a downpour, and he could no longer see ten feet in front of him. He stopped his horse and conceded to the inclement weather.

He stopped and made camp the best he could. He would have to spend a soggy, unpleasant night before getting back to his warm and inviting home. There was no way to escape the undeniable fact. One cold, rain-drenched night would separate him from his new family.

As a bounty hunter, he'd endured this and worse. Sleeping outdoors was nothing new. He was accustomed to the elements. No one cared about his coming or going, much less if he slept outdoors in the rain. The conditions hadn't troubled him.

That was before.

Now he was a family man. He had a home. Best of all, he had a wife and child waiting for him to return.

Chapter Twenty-Five
Freed, With a Child's Help

Caroline

Imprisoned in the dark cellar, Caroline did her best to quell her panic. The cellar was dank, cold, and home to a fair number of cobwebs. She shivered. The wind blew, gusting around the ranch house. The beams overhead creaked. The cold sent a deep chill across her skin, sinking to her bones. She rubbed her arms, trying to keep warm.

The darkness pressed against her like a shroud. Her heart drummed against her ribs. Her fear ebbed and flowed. When she grew fearful, blood rushed through her ears, drowning out other sounds, and she labored to draw a proper breath.

Slowly, she regained some semblance of calm. Her turmoil slowed. She took stock of her predicament. It wasn't good. She was stuck, perhaps for a good while. With Nick gone, it was just her and Annie. The girl wouldn't realize she was trapped in the cellar.

Summoning her wits, she ascended the narrow stairs, stopping at the top to bang on the overhead door with the palm of her hand. A dull thud reverberated across the thick span of wood. Annie would have to be nearby to hear the dull sound. In no time, her hand hurt painfully, and she abandoned her scheme.

She returned to her perch on the steps and shivered as the wind blew intermittently overhead. For a long while, she sat, racking her mind for a solution. She heard no sound from the house. A wave of unease came over her. Where was Annie. Was she safe?

An eerie silence followed. Even the wind had stilled. The only sound came from a soft scuffling in a corner of the cellar, a mouse, perhaps. Caroline didn't give it much thought. Her main concerns revolved around Annie. Was the child all right? The more Caroline pondered the question, and the more she endured the heavy silence, the more she fretted.

As the day passed, she tried time and again to get the child's attention. She shouted. She banged on the door. In the darkness, she found a broom which she used to both hammer the door and attempt to pry the door open. Nothing came of her efforts.

The minutes ticked past, turning into long hours. At times the wind whistled around the house. Other times she could hardly detect a gentle breeze. All the while, she shivered with the cold. Her desperation rose and fell. She'd imagine all sorts of awful scenarios, and just as quickly, she'd talk herself down.

Where was the child? She prayed Annie was safe, warm and sheltered inside the home, perhaps with Pumpkin as she read her beloved books.

The girl was capable enough. Caroline tried to reassure herself, recalling how Nick tasked Annie with various chores around the ranch. Annie made a point of doing Nick's tasks promptly and without complaint. Not like the small chores Caroline requested help with. Just the same, Annie was responsible and reliable.

Caroline would try to keep that in mind. Then her doubts would creep in. She'd imagine Annie, see her in her mind, so small, so young, so vulnerable.

For a nine-year old girl, Annie was strong. But like any nine-year old, she was fragile too. She tried to be tough to hide her vulnerability. Caroline saw the girl's defenselessness. She saw it in quiet moments when Annie wasn't aware. Perhaps Caroline recognized the child's vulnerability so keenly because Caroline had been an orphan too. She knew well the burden orphans silently endured, the unspoken unease, an expectation that their entire world, everything they'd ever known, could again disappear in the blink of an eye.

As the day wore on, Caroline tried time and again to call Annie but to no avail. The cold made her teeth chatter, especially when the wind picked up. She exhausted herself trying to get the girl's attention. After some time had passed, she fell asleep on the rough planks of the stairs.

Dreams flitted through her mind, images of Nick on the shore, the day they'd met. The sound of his laugh, a gentle rumble that would make his shoulders shake with sheer happiness. Annie's endless questions about anything and everything. The girl's curiosity was endless. In her dreams, Caroline could picture the girl's expression and hear the innocent tone of her voice. Sweet Annie.

Caroline awoke with a start, unsure where she was. It took a moment or two. Slowly, she understood the reality of her situation. She was trapped, shivering in the darkness, imprisoned deep in the cellar.

She rose and stretched, trying to ease the knots from her shoulders.

Her thoughts drifted to Nick. She missed him desperately. If he were home, he would have found her immediately. She realized this with a rush of warmth and appreciation. Even when Nick worked out in the back pastures, he'd seek her out the moment he returned. Always with a smile, or a sweet offer to help her with her tasks.

"Nick," she whispered. "How I miss you."

It pained her to think back on the time he'd tried to take her hand or talked about dancing with her. She'd refused his touch and dismissed his offer of dancing. Why? Because of pride. She feared he might find her lacking. She'd refused to believe he saw more in her than she saw in herself.

How she wished he were here now. She'd take his hand in *both* of hers. She'd hold on fast. She'd ask him to show her how to dance. She'd risk looking foolish and hope for the best, come what may. She'd try to be the wife he seemed to want and the wife he surely deserved.

Heaven help me.

More silence followed. Not even the mouse made a sound. And in a moment of clarity, it dawned on her she had tried everything she could to escape the cellar except prayer. She'd neglected to seek the Lord's help. She rubbed her forehead as dismay washed over her. A foolish, prideful error. The same mistake she made more often than she cared to admit.

When she found herself in trouble, she overlooked the solution she ought to seek first. It happened regularly. When faced with a dire problem, she'd do everything she could to solve the matter on her own. She'd struggle, she'd flail, rack her brain, then start the process all over again.

Mired in despair, she'd suddenly remember the one thing she overlooked. Prayer. Seeking the Lord's assistance or instruction. Much to her dismay, it happened almost every time she found herself in trouble.

She climbed the stairs and sat near the top step where she bowed her head and prayed in earnest.

Lord, save me from my own foolishness. I know I've...

"Caroline?" Annie's desperate words filtered through the cellar door.

"Annie?" Caroline's heart leapt. "Can you hear me?"

"I can hear you. Are you down there?"

Caroline stood, promptly banging her head on the same door. "Yes, Annie. I'm here."

"I was looking for you," the child cried. "Everywhere. In the house. The garden. The barn."

"I'm here," Caroline said again. She laughed, a light, nervous laugh of relief. "Are you all right?"

"Yes. I'm fine." A moment of silence ensued. "Pumpkin is fine too."

"I'm so glad." Caroline's legs gave way. She collapsed to the step where she'd been sitting. The immense relief was more than anything she'd ever known. Never before had she struggled with such deep dread. The notion that Annie might face some threat or danger, and that she'd be powerless to protect the child was more than she could fathom.

"We need to get you out," Annie said.

Caroline's frantic thoughts calmed. Her heart slowed. "Yes. We do need to find a way."

"I was looking for you," Annie said once more, this time her voice even and matter of fact.

"Were you?" Caroline smiled despite her predicament.

"Yes, ma'am. I looked everywhere." Annie gave a breathless laugh. "Mama Hen."

Caroline laughed softly. Relief flooded her heart. *Thank you, Lord. Thank you.* "Did you miss me?"

"I did. I missed you. So much."

Caroline's breath caught in her throat. She set her hand over her heart. Tears stung her eyes.

"I'm hungry." Annie's tone had a little of the old stubbornness.

Caroline's lips tugged into a tearful smile. She wasn't entirely sure how she'd escape the cellar. She might remain in the depths of the cellar for a good while. But the girl was safe and accounted for. Caroline sighed, overcome with a rush of unabashed love for the small girl.

She set her hands on her hips. "You might be hungry, Sassy Chick, but I'm trapped. I can't open the cellar door and I doubt you can either."

"No. No, ma'am."

Caroline tried to shake the fears that lingered. "I suppose we'll need to wait till Nick gets home."

Her heart thudded heavily to think she could remain in the cellar for a day or more. She'd manage, but Annie would be left unattended. Annie might be a capable girl, but she was still too young to be left alone. Meanwhile, the night stretched out before them both along with all the accompanying uncertainty.

Annie spoke. "You could crawl out the window."

"What window?"

"Make your way past the potatoes and turnips. Go down the narrow passage by the cornmeal bins. There's a window at the end of the little corridor."

Caroline descended the steps. When she reached the bottom, a jolt of pain struck her old injury. She paused, waiting for her leg to give her its usual trouble. But, for some reason, the pain subsided. She stood firmly upright and steadier than she'd ever stood in her life.

Drawing a fortifying breath, she proceeded slowly and cautiously. She held out her hands to feel her way around the bushels of produce and sacks of grain. Cobwebs lined the passage. She had to stop to brush them away. They sent a shudder of disgust through her, but she persisted. With each step, she drew nearer to the small passage Annie spoke of.

There was no light to guide her. Annie spoke of a window. If there was a window, wouldn't she see some small glimmer? She forged ahead, despite her misgivings, down the uneven path and utter darkness.

Something scurried in the darkness behind her. The mouse, she supposed. Worries flitted through her mind. Once, as a child, a mouse scampered across her bare foot as she prepared for bed. It raced across the orphanage bedroom, making every girl scream in terror. They'd all jumped atop their beds. She couldn't remember what happened after that, but the memory had endured.

Lord, help me find my way. And keep that mouse far away.

A thud drew her attention. From the end of the passage, something banged, sending a resounding thump across the still, dank air of the cellar. As she made her way, the sound grew louder.

"Caroline," Annie called, her voice muffled. "Can you hear me?"

"I can hear you." Caroline's voice choked with emotion. "I'm coming."

She pushed her way down the passage, moving past what felt like old feed sacks. She brushed aside various tools and implements that hung from the low ceiling. They clanged. The sound echoed in the darkness. With each step, she drew closer to the window. With each step, Annie's voice grew stronger.

When she reached the end of the passage, she heard Annie's voice once more. She reached up, past a dusty cobweb and found an assortment of burlap bundles. She shoved them aside. Light streamed through the murky window. Caroline squinted at the sudden brightness. Annie's face appeared. Even through the filthy window, Caroline could plainly see the girl was distraught.

"There you are!" Annie said plaintively. "I'm so happy to see you."

"I'm happy too. So happy."

Shelves lined the wall. Caroline set her foot on the bottom shelf. It was her weak leg. She drew a deep breath and pushed past the weakness, rising to the dim light above. The window was held fast by a small, rusty clasp. She tried to twist the handle, but it held fast.

"We can do it," Annie shouted. She pounded on the outside latch with a rock.

Caroline grabbed a short piece of lumber from the top shelf. She began working on the stubborn latch from the inside while Annie did her best on her side of the window. Together, they struck the latch with all their might, doing their best to loosen the old, unused latch. To Caroline's amazement, it began to give way. At first it was barely noticeable, but with each blow, it turned a little more. Finally, she and Annie managed to wrench it loose.

The moment the latch gave way, Annie shoved the window open. The window swung wide. Annie reached her hand through the opening, grabbed Caroline's hand, and burst into tears.

Caroline could hardly blame her. She wanted to weep as much as Annie. Perhaps more so. She managed to keep her wits about her as she pulled herself up and out the small window. The moment she was free, Annie clasped her arms around her middle and sobbed. The child trembled. Caroline's heart wrenched.

"It's fine," Caroline murmured, stroking the child's head. "It's all fine."

"I thought you were dead."

Caroline drew a sharp breath. Dead? Poor Annie. As much as Caroline had suffered, trapped in the cellar, Annie had endured her own private misery. Caroline embraced the girl and kissed the top of her head.

So many of Annie's ornery ways came from her fears. Caroline had seen the very same things play out in the orphanage. People liked to say children were resilient. But were they? Or was that simply the wishful thinking of adults?

No, children were tenderhearted and suffered as much as anyone else. They weren't always as resilient as adults hoped. In fact, many children were quite fragile. Even if they acted as if they were tough. Perhaps *especially* if they pretended to be strong.

"I'm going to make you a nice dinner, my little sassy chick," Caroline murmured. "Anything you want."

Annie's crying gave way to quiet. She looked up at Caroline with teary eyes. "Anything?"

"Anything."

"May I..." Annie's words drifted off. She swallowed hard. "May I have pancakes? If I promise to help? And to set the table?"

Caroline smiled. She stroked her fingers across Annie's forehead then brushed away the child's tears. "Of course, you can have pancakes. Anything you want. Anything at all."

Chapter Twenty-Six
In the Nick of Time

Nick

Nick was awake before daybreak and started the long ride home. It was muddy and slow-going, but he refused to wait any longer. He wanted to get home today.

With an hour to go, and little sunlight left in the day, his horse changed his gait. He was clearly bothered by something. Nick stopped and discovered a shoe had come loose. He cursed his bad luck and removed the shoe, then continued on foot to his cousin Paul's ranch, just a mile away. Paul would have the proper tools to get him back in the saddle.

This would add an hour to his day, but it couldn't be helped. At least he could still make it home today, and he could tell Caroline about the cattle he'd purchased and the gifts that would be along soon. He smiled thinking about how Caroline would react, and it pleased him to no end.

Twenty minutes later, Paul and Emmaline's house came into view. The place looked deserted, which made sense – most cowboys were taking part in the fall roundup. It'd be a few more days before they all returned.

Nick hesitated, unsure if he wanted to bother Emmaline this late in the day. He didn't want to startle her right before dark. Given his options, he decided to go straight to the barn to reshoe his horse, as quietly as he could. He doubled down on his decision when he realized he'd save himself at least fifteen minutes by not knocking on the front door, what with the conversation and visiting that would surely be expected. No, he'd do what he needed and be on his way.

In the dim light inside the barn, he found a tack hammer and shoe nails and was just about to grab the horse's leg, when he heard some yipping noises come from a stall. He opened the barn door further to get some light, and in the stall, he found a large, white dog and four wriggly, fuzzy puppies.

Nick squatted and held out his hand, as if he had something interesting to offer. The mama didn't budge, but one of the furrballs bounded over to him and sniffed his hand, then awkwardly pranced around him, ready to play. Nick reached to scratch the little one behind the ears, but the mama didn't approve of that.

She stood up quickly and in an instant was between Nick and her baby. She did not growl or bark, but she made it clear that she did not appreciate Nick in her house.

"Well, look at you," Nick said. "You are a handsome girl." Nick reached his hand out to the mama, keeping it a foot away from her and near the ground. The dog leaned forward and sniffed him. For a dog, two sniffs are as good as a handshake. Once Nick offered his hand, the mama was satisfied, and she sat down in front of him, staring at him with her black eyes. Nick reached and scratched her behind the ear, and she leaned into it, clearly appreciating his touch.

The four pups surrounded him, bumping each other to put their paws on him, their short tails wagging. He made sure to stroke each one of them, and a thought came to mind. Annie wanted a dog, and he liked the looks of these, very much. First chance he got, he planned to ask Paul if he could buy one from him.

The pups were fun, and he could have spent more time playing with them, but it was late, and he wanted to get home. As he returned to his horse, he heard a window crash at the house. He rushed out of the barn and heard a stranger's voice coming from the house, yelling something he could not make out. Emmaline was in trouble. He bolted, running full speed toward the house.

When he reached the house, everything had gone silent. He slowed his breath and listened, trying to surmise what was going on. After a few seconds he decided to call out Emmaline's name, but just before he did the front door flew open and Emmaline rushed out and down the steps. Before Nick could speak, another figure came bursting through the door, a man with a gun in his hand. Neither of them saw Nick.

"Get back here, you wench!"

Nick wasted no time. He ran straight at the man and drove him to the ground, dislodging the man's gun. When he fell to the ground, the man cracked his head against a mesquite stump. Mesquite is the hardest wood in Texas, as hard as iron, and the blow rendered the man unconscious.

Nick saw he was still breathing but could tell he'd be out for a good while. Thankfully. It was tough to make out the man's features due to his rough beard, but after a moment, Nick realized the man was a crook he'd met before. Long ago. It was Jack Masterson, a carriage thief he'd collared down by Houston several years prior.

Nick turned to check on Emmaline, only to find she had picked up the pistol and was pointing it straight at his head.

"Whoa now, Emmaline. It's me, Nick McCord."

She paled. "Oh my..."

With that, she collapsed to the ground in a heap.

Nick rushed over to Emmaline and took the gun from her hand. Eyes closed, white as new milk, Emmaline was breathing and showed no sign of injury, thankfully. He tucked the gun in his belt and then returned to the crook. Why this man was on Paul's ranch, Nick had no idea, but he wanted to make sure he didn't wake up and escape.

Nick fetched a rope from the barn and tied the man up, as tightly as he could, unconcerned if the man could still breathe or not. In all his days as a bounty hunter he'd never felt as angry as he did now. The idea that anyone would try to hurt one of his own kin was more than he could tolerate. He nearly just shot the man there on the ground, but he refrained from doing so, honoring the oath he took so long ago when he first became a lawman.

You enforce the laws. You don't make them. And you don't decide who lives and dies.

Once the villain was fully secured Nick returned to Emmaline and carried her inside. He set her on a couch and brought her a glass of water. She opened her eyes soon enough and was at first panicked, but she quickly settled once Nick explained that everything was under control.

She took a sip of water and set the glass down, her hand trembling. "He said he was looking for you, Nick."

"Come again?"

"He said you'd done him wrong, and it was time for him to pay you back."

Nick's thoughts spun. When Nick hauled Jack Masterson to jail, Jack was an outlaw, to be sure, but he wasn't a killer, or at least Nick didn't think he was. He'd been sent to prison. Men could change while incarcerated, sometimes for the better, sometimes not.

"I met the man once, shortly after he robbed a coach near Houston. The judge found him guilty. I suppose he served his sentence. Either that or he escaped. Why or how he figured to hunt me down, I do not know."

Emmaline stood up and went to the kitchen to get more water. Nick followed her, watching how she moved to make sure she had her wits about her again. She did, apparently, because she offered to make him a coffee and feed him.

Nick glanced out the window to check on Jack Masterson. Thankfully, the scoundrel was still out cold, sprawled in the dirt.

"I'm not hungry. Thank you."

Nick was about to insist Emmaline come home with him. Caroline would tend to the poor woman until Paul returned. Before he could say as much, Paul and another horseman rode up to the ranch house. Nick didn't recognize the other man, but soon learned the stranger was the new sheriff of Bethany Springs.

Adam Kendall seemed like a strong, upstanding fellow, a fine lawman. He made short work of hauling off Jack Masterson. He tossed the unconscious outlaw over the back of one of Paul's mules and retied his hands and feet for good measure.

When Sheriff Kendall left, Nick and Paul spoke of the day's events. Paul looked almost as shaken as Emmaline had a short while before. As Nick recounted the story, Paul was rendered speechless with shock and dismay. Emmaline came to his side and wrapped her arms around him.

"I best be off," Nick said quietly. "I'm eager to see my wife and daughter, especially in light of what happened here."

"Thank the good Lord you were here," Paul said.

"My horse lost a shoe. I made myself at home in your barn and used your tools. I figured you wouldn't mind."

Paul shook his head, still overcome with emotion.

Emmaline answered on his behalf. "Of course not. We're family."

"That we are," Nick replied. Suddenly a wash of warmth came over him. Maybe it was seeing how affected Paul was by the day's events and how close his wife had come to harm. In the past, Nick had fretted day and night about Annie's safety. Now he, too, had a wife to protect. His mouth went dry. Suddenly he missed Caroline with all his heart. He yearned to be on his way, more than ever.

He prepared to take his leave and be on his way.

"Did you see the puppies?" Emmaline asked.

It took Nick a moment to recall the litter of pups in the barn. He smiled and nodded. "Mighty handsome dogs."

"I've heard all about your little Annie," Emmaline said kindly. "She's doing her best to collect as many animals as she can."

"Yes, ma'am. It's true."

"The pups are ready to leave their mama. Why not pick one out for Annie."

"She'd be mighty pleased to have one."

"I know she'll take good care of it," Emmaline replied. "It would be going to a fine home."

Paul seemed to recover his senses. He scrubbed a hand down his face and nodded. "Go on. Those Great Pyrenees are the finest ranch dog you can find. Take your choice. You'll have the pick of the litter."

Nick couldn't help grinning at the prospect of returning with such a pretty little pup. Annie would be overjoyed. He tipped his hat. "Much obliged."

With that, he bid them goodbye, with a few words about seeing them soon at Sophie and Robert's home for a wedding celebration. A short while later, Nick was riding home with a new pup nestled in the crook of his arm.

Chapter Twenty-Seven
A Joyful Reunion

Caroline

Nighttime settled around the ranch house. One more night without Nick. Caroline tucked Annie into bed, praying with her beforehand, then telling her a story to help settle her down to sleep. Almost every night, Annie wanted a story from Caroline. Not a story from a book. Certainly not a story that included a stepmother, but a story that Caroline came up with as they sat together.

Caroline complied. She was pleased to share quiet moments at the end of the day with the small girl. It seemed particularly special with Nick gone. She and Annie had forged a special bond, especially after the ordeal in the cellar.

They both missed Nick tremendously, Annie every bit as much as Caroline.

Caroline sat on the edge of Annie's bed and stroked Pumpkin's head as she told Annie a bedtime story. The child lay beneath the blankets, snuggled in her warm bed as the wind stirred around the ranch house. The cold, gusting wind made the evening seem especially lonesome.

Nick should be home tomorrow, or the day after that at the latest. Caroline did her best to school her thoughts and remain cheerful. She refused to fret. It wouldn't do her or Annie any good.

On the bright side of things, at least Caroline had managed to escape the dreaded depths of the cellar. She and Annie had enjoyed sweet moments of closeness since then. They'd baked two cakes. They'd practiced crocheting and Caroline was pleased to see the girl's progress. Together they'd swept the entire house, the front and back porch, as well as hauled several loads of firewood inside.

All the while, Caroline and Annie had talked about everything under the sun. Caroline spoke of her life in Boston, her trip to Texas on the Liberty, and the shipwreck. She also described her childhood memories of the orphanage, most of them quite pleasant, much to Annie's surprise.

The bedtime story that night was about a shoemaker and his kittens, a rendition of a well-known tale with a slight variation. It was just the sort of thing that delighted the girl. Anytime Annie was delighted, Caroline was too.

Annie's lids drooped. She looked close to sleep. Caroline paused her story. Outside the wind grew stronger, banging a nearby shutter. She held her breath, waiting to see if Annie was indeed off to sleep, but no, the child wasn't ready. Not yet.

Annie's eyes flew wide. "I'm awake! What happens to the orphaned kittens?"

Caroline smiled. She smoothed the blankets across Annie's bed and proceeded with her story. Pumpkin, meanwhile, bumped her head against Caroline's hand, purring loudly. Caroline went on with her tale, making up the details as she went along.

"The kittens, you see, weren't used to wearing shoes." Caroline stifled a yawn. "They knew nothing about how to tie their laces."

Annie nodded. "It's hard. It took me a long time."

Caroline patted her hand. "Me too."

Annie patted her hand in response. "And we have fingers. Imagine how hard it is with paws."

"Indeed."

"And they had four little boots. Not two like you and me."

"I hadn't thought of that." Caroline laughed softly. "No wonder they had trouble." She stroked Pumpkin's head. "Poor Pumpkin. If he ever wants boots, we'll be sure to help tie all four of his laces, won't we, Annie?"

The girl's face lit with pure delight at the absurd notion of her kitten wearing boots. Caroline had the suspicion neither Nick nor Aunt Penny ever indulged in such playful, outlandish notions. She was more than a little pleased to share such a moment with Annie. To Caroline, quiet moments like this were gifts from God.

"Thank you, Caroline," the girl murmured.

"For what?"

"For the story. The cakes. Everything you do."

Caroline smiled. "I'm pleased to do those things for you. I never imagined having a sweet little girl to care for. I never imagined having a family."

Annie knit her brow. "Why not?"

"Why not?" Caroline drew a deep breath and considered her reply and how much to share with the girl.

"Didn't you want a family?"

"I did. Very much. But I was injured as a child."

Annie's lips parted with surprise. "What happened to you?"

"I hurt my leg. Badly."

"Oh, no!"

"It never really healed properly. Ever since, I've walked... unevenly." Caroline couldn't bear to refer to her gait as a limp. She refused to say the word aloud. It had always pained her to hear the doctors use the word with such a casual and dismissive air.

"Your leg, is it still sore?" Annie propped herself up on an elbow and peered over the edge of her bed at Caroline's boots as if expecting to see some evidence of the old injury.

Suddenly, self-conscious, Caroline smoothed her hands over her skirts and tugged them down to conceal her boots. "No. Not anymore."

Annie lay back on her pillow a slight crease between her eyes.

"I've made a point to strengthen my legs," Caroline explained. "Ever since I left Boston, in fact."

Her chest felt tight. As much as she wished to speak openly with the girl, the discussion bothered her a great deal. It was only a matter of time before Annie told Nick. And then they'd both know of her past.

"I never noticed anything wrong." Annie shrugged her shoulder.

Caroline could hardly believe her ears. Was it possible that Annie, like Nick, hadn't noticed? It couldn't be. All her life, Caroline had battled the old injury. Through the years, she'd desperately tried to conceal her uneven gait. Things changed when she'd boarded the Liberty. Not right away, of course. It took time and daily exercise on the ship's deck. As the days passed, she dared hope that she was making progress.

Since arriving in Texas, she'd grown stronger each day. And yet, she secretly fretted that any day, either Annie or Nick would confront her about the shortcoming.

After all that worry, Annie hadn't noticed.

Caroline couldn't hold back a breathless laugh. Her mind returned to the time Nick had told her those very words. It happened the day she'd ventured down to the barn to ask him to mend her boot. He asked why she needed to adjust the heel. She hinted at her injury. He claimed to *hardly notice*. Just like Annie.

Caroline didn't believe him that day. No, she assumed that Nick was merely being polite. Not so with Annie. The girl concealed nothing. Annie was a girl who spoke her mind. She would have told Caroline outright if she'd ever observed a limp.

"I'm so pleased you didn't notice," Caroline said, hoping she wouldn't grow teary-eyed. "That might be the nicest thing anyone has ever told me."

Annie looked bewildered. Of course, she did. The child had suffered more than her share of loss but hadn't lived with a lifelong injury. Thank goodness.

A sound came from the parlor. The door opened. Wind gusted and blew down the hallway, ruffling Annie's curtains. Caroline drew a sharp breath. Annie's lips parted with surprise. Even Pumpkin was startled by the unexpected intrusion.

Nick called through the house. "Hello, McCord family!"

Annie gasped. She threw back the blankets and bolted from her bed.

A shimmer of happiness washed over Caroline. Nick was home. The news felt like the comfort of a warm blanket on a winter's night.

She rose and followed Annie down the hallway. When she reached the doorway and caught her first glimpse of Nick, she stopped in her tracks to take in the sight of her husband. Nick stood in the doorway, completely disheveled, muddy and unshaven. Clad in his rough ranch coat, rumpled shirt, vest, trousers, and boots.

"Uncle Nick," Annie cried throwing her arms around his waist.

He hugged Annie back and planted a kiss atop her head. "Sweet girl. I bought you a present."

"You did? Candy?"

"Better than candy." He winked at Caroline.

Warmth drifted the length of her neck and sent a flush across her face. Try as she might, she couldn't tear her eyes from Nick. She'd missed him more than she cared to admit. She felt like a fool, staring at him. She'd learned as a child that staring was bad manners. And while she took pride in her manners, she couldn't stop herself.

Summoning some bit of sense, she spoke. "It's good to see you, Nick."

He nodded, a roguish grin curving his lips. "It's good to see you, darlin'."

Another wave of awkwardness rushed over her, warming her heart, and making it race. She sighed. He'd called her darling. His voice was deep, kind and warm. The endearment made her happier than she could imagine. Such a small word. And yet, it conveyed more than she'd ever dreamed of.

He turned his attention to Annie, who clamored to know what he'd brought her. He stepped back outside and whistled. A moment later a pup bounded inside. It scampered around the parlor, knocking over a small side table and crashing into the chairs.

Annie gasped with surprise and delight. She knelt down and called the pup. It dashed back across the room and wriggled with excitement as Annie cooed and murmured soft words. The pup lay down and promptly rolled over to offer his belly.

Pumpkin strolled into the room and stopped abruptly. He glared at the small, wriggling intruder. Instantly, he retreated several steps, hissed and arched his back.

"What do you think, Pumpkin?" Annie asked.

"Not much from the looks of things," Nick said.

Caroline nodded. "I think you're right."

Nick smiled, set his hat on a nearby table, patted his hair and crossed the room. A pace or so away from her, he stopped abruptly. His smile faltered. Clearing his throat, he spoke. "Nice to see you."

"Nice to see you," Caroline replied softly.

Nick kept a slight distance, as if waiting for an invitation to come closer. That had been his way up till now, respectful of her wishes. Still, she could tell he yearned to draw near. He shifted from one foot to the other. He cleared his throat once more. He shoved his hands in his pockets. Then, thinking better, he took them out and clasped before him.

Caroline decided to end his discomfort. She stepped closer and took his hands in hers. She heard his sharp breath. He gazed down at her, a distinct note of confusion in his eyes. His surprise gave way to a small smile.

"I'm so glad," Caroline said softly.

"You are?"

"I am."

Caroline had meant to say more, that she was not just glad, but more to the point, glad that he was *home*. As the silence stretched between them, she saw plainly he'd taken a different meaning to her words entirely. He'd understood her to say she was glad not just that he'd returned, but about everything. The letters someone else had written. The misunderstanding. The marriage neither of them had expected.

"I am glad," she said quietly. "About everything."

"Me too," he said softly.

He wrapped his arms around her waist and coaxed her closer to him. She complied, allowing him to draw her into his arms. He traced his fingers along her jaw and lifted her chin. Slowly and tenderly, he lowered to kiss her lips. Caroline met his kiss as she wrapped her arms around his neck.

"Wait a minute," Annie exclaimed.

Caroline broke the kiss and took a half-step back. Nick smiled down at her. He kept his warm gaze fixed on her and held her in the circle of his arms. After a moment, he turned away to speak to Annie.

"What is it, Little Bit?" Nick growled good naturedly.

"Did you bring Mama Hen a present?"

"I did," he answered. "Indeed."

"Please tell me it's not a puppy," Caroline murmured.

He gave a small shake of his head.

"What did you bring her?" Annie asked.

"I didn't bring them with me, but someone will bring them next week," he replied. "If she wants them, that is."

"What?" said both girls together.

"A sewing machine and a loom."

"A sewing machine? And a loom? Truly?" Caroline asked.

"Truly," Nick replied.

Caroline hadn't expected anything, much less such a fine gift. Singer sewing machines were very dear and not a trivial sort of gift. And looms were also a big investment. "Thank you." He held her closer.

A moment later, she added, "It's a lovely surprise." She stole a glance in his direction. "All I really wanted was for my husband to return."

"I'm back, sweetheart." He pulled her closer and kissed the top of her head. "This is all I wanted too. Just to return home to my unexpected bride."

Chapter Twenty-Eight
A Moonlit Dance

Nick

Sophie McCord sent out invitations far and wide. On the last Saturday in October, Sophie and Robert would host a dinner and dance in celebration of Nick and Caroline's marriage. Word was that more than a hundred friends and family had been invited. Nick didn't know what he thought about such a large gathering, but he didn't worry about it too much. So long as he was with Caroline, he didn't care how big the party was.

"We ought to dance a time or two, and practice a bit before the big shindig," he told Caroline one evening after Annie had gone to bed.

The house was quiet. Peaceful. It was his favorite time of the day when he and Caroline were alone, and they had a chance to visit and get to know one another a little more each day.

He awaited her answer, wondering what she'd have to say about the notion of dancing with him. When she didn't reply, he eyed her, and kept his attention on her as he waited for a response. None followed. No. Caroline didn't say a word. Instead, she continued writing a letter to her friend, Beth. She'd told him she intended to invite Beth and her husband to

Sophie and Robert's party. Finally, Caroline stopped writing and lifted her gaze to meet his as she considered her reply.

He sat across the parlor, mending a pair of reins by the light of the fire. Various animals slept in the periphery. Pumpkin lay curled on a nearby chair. The pup that Annie named Percy, for some reason, dozed on a blanket near the fire. Percy was a round circle of fluff, his nose tucked beneath his tail, likely trying to fend off the early autumn chill.

Nick stopped his work, wondering if she might allow him to take her into his arms at Sophie's party. Might she permit him to lead her into a dance? His heart raced at the thought. It would be their first as man and wife before their friends and family.

Caroline's lips curved into the hint of a smile. "From the sounds of things, we're expected to dance at Aunt Sophie's party. Why not wait till then?"

She went back to writing. He could see that she hoped he'd let the matter rest. She was still shy at times, especially when it came to matters pertaining to marriage. While he was eager to proceed with their marriage bond, she remained decidedly reticent. Still, he felt some degree of satisfaction. Day by day, the distance between them narrowed.

It had been just a few weeks since he'd left Annie and Caroline to buy cattle in Comal County. His trip had been more eventful than anyone expected, what with stumbling upon the outlaw, Jack Masterson. Thankfully, that incident had turned out well. No one was hurt, except the crook, and he was behind bars again, where he belonged.

On the home front, he'd encountered a welcome change. Ever since he'd returned, Caroline had seemed warmer, more settled. Why, she even allowed him to take her hand in his. Just this morning, he'd brushed a kiss across the top of her hand. It had earned him a lovely pink blush from his sweet bride.

"Maybe you don't need to practice, but I'm mite rusty. A few minutes of dancing might help me feel more confident about it," he said, teasing gently.

Caroline replied without hesitation, with her own gently teasing tone. "I've hardly ever danced, as you know. However, it seems people usually have some music to dance to. Isn't that how things are done?"

"Not necessarily."

She looked up. "Beg your pardon?"

"I'll hum a tune. And I'll count for you, so you understand the cadence."

"Hum and count? At the same time?"

He chuckled. "I'm very talented. What's more, there's a full moon. What do you say we try a few steps on the porch. I get nervous practicing in front of a crowd."

"Really?"

"Really."

"I wonder what Juliet Williams would say to that."

He winced as he tried not to grin. He disliked how Juliet had acted so haughty when he'd introduced Caroline and explained that he'd married. On the other hand, it pleased him that Caroline felt some small degree of jealousy. Heaven knows he'd be far more jealous if the shoe were on the other foot. Just the same, it felt like progress. Caroline wanted him all to herself and that was more than fine by him.

He set the needle, thread, and reins aside and got to his feet. "I never danced with her, Caroline."

"Ah, yes. That's right. She seemed disappointed." Caroline said.

"I didn't want to dance with her. You know why?" he asked crossing the room to stop a pace from the dining table.

"Why?"

"Because I was waiting for you."

She didn't reply. Instead, she gazed up at him, a soft expression in her eyes. He held out his hand and beckoned her. When she remained seated, he circled the table and drew her out of the chair and led her outside onto the porch.

Silver moonlight cast a soft glow across the surroundings. The night was still. Stars twinkled across the sky.

Taking her hand in his, he drew her closer. She looked up at him, with an uneasy expression. Even after all the time they'd spent together, now close to a month, Caroline was still so unsure. At times he blamed the mystery matchmaker for Caroline's reticence.

Whenever that happened, he was quick to remind himself that the same mystery matchmaker, whoever it was, had brought him and Caroline together. With that in mind, he quickly dismissed every one of his complaints. He'd make certain to court his bride and would take his time if that was what she needed.

"You're the dance partner I waited for," he said gently. "Now, let's see if I can show you a step or two without music."

He drew her closer and counted under his breath as he led her into a simple two-step. She was as stiff as a fence post. She stepped on his foot, then stumbled. After that, she seemed hesitant to move at all.

He ignored her missteps and alternated between humming softly and counting, one, two, one, two, three. For such a tiny, slender, and delicate woman, Caroline wasn't the easiest dance partner. Even without knowing the steps, she felt heavy and clumsy.

Despite the missteps, he carried on as if she danced perfectly, humming and counting, moving her across the porch, in and out of the moonlight. As much as anything, he loved the feel of her in his arms. He relished her sweet floral scent, and the softness of her hand. He didn't care if she stepped on his toes or bumped into his chest. Just so long as he could hold her close.

When she stepped on his boot for the umpteenth time, she let out a soft murmur of dismay.

"Nothing to worry about, sweetheart," he said softly, spinning her as he counted.

"I'm terrible," she grumbled under her breath.

He stopped. She crashed against his chest and looked up, her expression etched with disappointment and self-rebuke.

"Don't say that, Caroline. You're not terrible. Besides it doesn't matter."

"It doesn't?"

"Course not. The important thing is that you and I dance together. Don't worry about what it looks like. What matters is what's happening here." He tapped his chest. "This is what matters when a man dances with his bride. What's happening in his heart. And hers too."

She swallowed and nodded silently.

"You feel it in your heart?" he asked.

"Yes, very much."

"Me too." He smiled. "And that's the important thing."

A soft breath escaped her parted lips. He lowered slowly, with deliberate gentle movement and brushed his lips across hers. Her kiss was soft. Her lips invited him to linger. He half expected her to bolt like a frightened doe. Instead, she gave herself over to his kiss. She sank into his embrace. To his delight and surprise, she wrapped her arms around his neck.

When they drew back, he looked at her with the same wonder with which she regarded him. The glow of moonlight lit her lovely face. The sight of her in his arms made his heart skip a beat. Maybe two or three. He hardly cared. The only thing that mattered was that she'd danced with him. That and the simple fact she'd finally let him gather her in his arms and draw her into his embrace.

Little by little he was making progress.

For that he thanked the Lord. A verse from Proverbs came to mind. *Be patient and gentle with one another, avoiding arguments and pride.*

He'd do that and more, he vowed silently. That and more. For his family, the one he hadn't expected, but the one given to him with God's providence, he'd do that and more.

Chapter Twenty-Nine
Sophie's Shindig

Nick

The first days of October had turned warm and felt almost as hot as August. Folks were ready for some cooler weather. Thankfully, the weather changed by and by. All with God's perfect timing was what Aunt Penny used to say. Mornings dawned a little cooler. Rain came and went, leaving a chill in its wake. Evenings and nights were cool or sometimes downright cold.

Nick hadn't ever been bothered by the change of seasons, but he'd never had a wife before either. He appreciated the cooler weather and especially how Caroline felt in his arms whenever she sensed a chill in the air and sought warmth in his embrace. For a Boston girl, his wife seemed mighty disinclined towards the cold. Suited him just fine. He was happy to hold her day or night.

The morning of Sophie's party dawned still and unseasonably warm, but by mid-afternoon, he sensed a blue northern was on its way. Typical Texas weather. The cold front would arrive sometime in the wee hours of the night, or that's what he guessed.

The morning was spent preparing for the celebration. Caroline and Annie both took long baths. After, they debated what to wear. When they'd finally decided on which dress they preferred, they debated various boot choices. Nick hadn't spent any time pondering such matters. After a quick bath, he'd simply put on his usual suit and boots. He kept busy while his wife and daughter got ready for the party.

After all was said and done, and they finally got to Robert and Sophie's home, he confided in the McCord brothers, telling them about the length of time it took for his wife and daughter to prepare for the shindig.

"Just three hours?" Paul asked. "That's nothing."

"Wait till you have a child," Ezra muttered. He took a sip of the fruit punch and eyed the guests gathered in the garden. "A child might be small and inconspicuous, but don't be fooled. The little ones require extra time. A simple trip to town is darned near as complicated as driving a thousand head of cattle to Abilene."

The men laughed and murmured their agreement.

Nick could hardly hold back a smile. Annie meant the world to him. And almost from the first moment he saw Caroline on the shore, he'd imagined more children. His wife was the blessing he never expected, and he prayed for more of the Lord's blessings. Slowly, and with patience, Nick had somehow convinced Caroline that the two of them were meant to be man and wife.

Over time, Caroline slowly welcomed and accepted the idea of a real marriage. Each night after they said goodnight to Annie, they'd fallen asleep together, wrapped in each other's arms. He hoped and prayed they'd be blessed with a child sometime next summer.

"I wanted to talk to you about something more serious," Paul McCord said quietly.

Nick waited and wondered. He fretted too, for he depended on the McCord brothers and the lease of Theo

McCord's ranch. His plans for his family depended on staying on Theo's land. In a few years he'd have enough to buy his own place, but for now, he had to borrow.

"Serious matters?" Nick asked casually.

"Yes, about Uncle Theo's ranch."

Nick didn't much care for the direction of this conversation. "Ok," he said with marked reluctance.

"You know about Uncle Theo's will, and the ridiculous requirement to name a child after him in order to inherit his homestead, right?"

"I do."

"Well, my wife is expecting a child just after the new year, and Ezra and Nate's wives are pregnant too. We figure one of us will likely have a new son before next spring."

"That's great news, Paul. Congratulations."

"Thank you. Point is, I've talked to my brothers, and we've all agreed that whoever is the first to be blessed with a boy will name that boy Theo."

Nick just looked at him, unsure where this was going.

"Once the boy's name is legal, the conditions of the will will be met, and ownership of Uncle Theo's ranch will be transferred to one of us three boys."

Nick just stared at Paul, unsure what to say.

"As soon as that happens, and we've all agreed on this, the ranch will be sold."

Nick tried to conceal his disappointment. "Who will you sell it to?" Nick asked.

Paul smiled, a warmth washing over his gaze. "To you."

Nick waited for Paul to say more. Part of him felt overwhelming relief. He'd have a chance to buy the ranch. It was everything he wanted. On the other hand, he probably couldn't pay his cousins what the ranch was worth. His heart sank. Despite his misgivings, he tried his best to offer Paul a cheerful smile.

"That's mighty nice," Nick said. "I appreciate it. Your family has been more than kind to me. I'm not sure-"

"The price will be three dollars," Paul said. With that, he patted Nick on the shoulder. "One dollar for each of us."

Nick was thunderstruck. "You're kidding me."

"Nope. We talked and there's no way we're letting you ever leave Bethany Springs. We intend to make things permanent. You saved my wife, and I can never repay you for that. You're a good man, with a fine family. We consider you our fourth brother, and we want you to stay here, forever."

"I don't know what to say."

"You don't need to say anything. Before the spring auction we'll take care of all the formalities and you will be the owner of a new ranch, Uncle Theo's fine homestead. Now, isn't it about time we started dancing? Where's my wife?"

Paul nodded and took his leave.

Nick stood rooted to the spot. His mind spun with this astonishing news. The ranch would be his. He'd worked hard, building fences and repairing barns, all the while wondering if his work would benefit him or the next owner. Now he knew. He'd own the land and the house.

Nick searched the crowd for Caroline. She stood next to Annie, talking to Sophie and Robert. He was about to join his wife and tell her the unexpected news when Adam Kendall, the new sheriff, came to his side.

Sheriff Kendall had hauled Jack Masterson off just a few weeks before.

They spoke for a short time about the outlaw. The sheriff had taken the man to Austin and left him with the Texas Rangers.

"No need to ever worry about Jack Masterson," Adam Kendall said. "He'll be behind bars till he's old and gray. Maybe longer."

"Much obliged," Nick said, eager to take his leave and join Caroline and Annie.

"Happy to help. I heard you weren't the one to send off for a missus."

Nick felt a jolt of surprise.

Adam Kendall carried on without a moment's worry. "Seems it turned out well. The new Mrs. McCord is mighty pretty and, from what I heard, a good cook. Look at how sweet she is with the little one. Everyone's saying that Annie's going to have a passel of critters before year's end."

A moment before, Nick had been ready to share the good news with Caroline about Uncle Theo's estate. In an instant that had changed. More than anything he wanted to protect Caroline from any rumors he hadn't sent for her. Sheriff Kendall's casual words hit him hard, and he was determined to shield Caroline from hearing any such comments.

"What do you mean by that?" Nick demanded.

Adam started counting off the various critters on his fingers. "Cats, dogs, chickens. Seems she wants a few donkeys and *turkeys* for some reason."

Nick lowered his voice. "I'm not talking about Annie or the animals she hopes to collect. How do you know I didn't send off for Caroline?"

Adam looked perplexed. "I don't know. Not exactly."

"You're the sheriff! You ought to know."

"It's nothing more than talk! People say this and that. You know how it is. You were a bounty hunter, weren't you?"

Nick shook his head. No, he didn't know how it was. As a bounty hunter he never acted on *this and that*. After a long moment, he spoke. "It's true. Someone in Bethany Springs sent letters on my behalf."

An awkward silence stretched between them. Nick spoke. "A matchmaker lurks in Bethany Springs. I'm not complaining, but I'll bet this person or persons will strike again."

Sheriff Kendall smiled and shrugged. "Worked out well for all parties. I don't intend to investigate. It was a gift to you, not a crime, that someone sent for your mail order bride. I don't investigate gifts."

Nick nodded. The sheriff didn't want to investigate. Suited him just fine. There might have been a time when he'd need to get to the bottom of matters, but he was long past his bounty hunter tendencies. He was no longer a lawman. That part of his life was over. In a surprisingly short time, he'd gone from hard-nosed lawman to grateful family man.

He was about to bid the sheriff goodbye.

"One thing is certain," Sheriff Kendall said. "I'm not concerned about your so-called matchmaker. I'm sure they acted on your behalf and don't have any further plans."

The two men shared a laugh. Nick took his leave and started to make a beeline to Caroline, but someone grabbed his arm from behind.

Robert McCord, Sophie's husband, released his grip on Nick's arm then opened his hand for a handshake. "Congratulations, young man," he said, beaming.

"Thank you, sir," Nick said, as the two men shared a firm handshake.

Another gentleman extended his hand as well.

"I'm Wade McCord, Robert's brother."

"Of course, you are Amelia Honeycutt's husband," Nick said while the men shook hands.

"Guilty as charged."

The men were quiet for a moment, and Nick, eager to get to Caroline, started to excuse himself, but Wade spoke before he could.

"I bet you were quite surprised when Caroline showed up in Galveston," Wade said.

Nick was exasperated. Was everyone going to talk about his bride and how she came to be in Texas? "Surprised and pleased," Nick said.

"Good, good. I'm really glad to hear that."

"Me too," Robert said. "It seems to me it was very risky for someone to write letters on your behalf, without your approval."

"That's right," Wade added. "It's a serious crime, assuming a false identity with the intent to defraud, although in this case I'm not sure the letters rise to the level of fraud, but I have to wonder if the people who wrote those letters realize the legal jeopardy they put themselves in."

"They?" Nick asked, stunned.

"Well, they, or she... or he," said Wade quickly. "Who knows, right?"

Robert's gaze went side-eye to Wade, while Wade smiled like the Cheshire cat from Alice in Wonderland.

"Looks like your lovely wife is looking for you," Robert said.

"Nice meeting you son," said Wade.

The two men turned and walked away together, talking and laughing as they made their way to the front porch.

Nick watched them intently, sure there was more to that conversation than he could understand. A tap on his shoulder changed his thoughts. Caroline stood a pace away, looking up at him with an expression that made his heart skip a few beats.

"There you are," she teased gently. "Here I thought I'd need to track down my bounty hunter husband."

A wash of warmth flowed over his heart. That morning he'd woken with the first rays of dawn. In his arms, Caroline lay, sleeping. She slept with her head on his shoulder. The feeling of her next to him was better than anything he knew. He could wake up with Caroline in his arms for the rest of eternity.

For now, he'd need to set those thoughts aside.

He kissed the top of Caroline's head. "You're tracking your bounty hunter husband? On what charges?"

She grinned, amusement lighting her eyes. "An outstanding account. A debt of a two-step."

"I owe a debt?" he countered. "And to whom do I owe this two-step?"

She laughed. "Your wife."

Before he could reply, she turned her attention to Annie who stood at her side. The girl smiled up at him, looking as lovely as a picture. Caroline had braided Annie's hair and tucked blossoms amidst the silk braids. Annie wore a gown that Caroline had sewed especially for this day. Annie's gown was a different color but matched Caroline's lace collar and cuffs. Caroline and Annie looked startlingly close to a mother and daughter pair.

The musicians began to play, a simple melody that was perfect for a Texas two-step.

A wash of pure contentment came over Nick. "I owe my wife a two-step," he murmured.

Caroline pulled Annie to her side. "Your wife and daughter."

It made no sense at all and yet it made perfect sense. He'd intended to tell Caroline all about the ranch, but for now he only wanted to feel her near. The news of the ranch could wait. The party was for them, to celebrate their marriage. He sensed the crowd gathering round and watching them. They likely expected him and Caroline to dance as a couple. Instead, he picked up Annie and held her in one arm and wrapped his other arm around his wife. He'd practiced dancing with Caroline and yet, for some reason, he yearned to take this first dance with not just Caroline but with Annie too.

"Love you both," he said softly.

His newfound family. The prayer he'd never prayed for.

The Lord's providence he never before imagined.

The End

Book Two of Bethany Springs Matchmakers
Mail Order Noelle

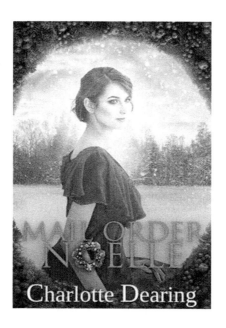

Texas Sheriff turned Family Man
Someone in Bethany Springs has a secret plot.

Adam Kendall is plenty busy. He's the sheriff of Bethany Springs, and he runs his family ranch. It's just him and his elderly grandfather, along with a couple of scrappy young ranch hands living on the Kendall ranch. Adam's life is full and he's sure that he's content.

Someone in Bethany Springs has plans for the bachelor sheriff. A surprise mail-order wife, who arrives a few weeks before Christmas. An unwelcome surprise turns out to be the gift of a lifetime.

Books by Charlotte Dearing

Mail Order Noelle
Mail Order Holly
Mail Order Sarah
Mail Order Ruth

Brides of Bethany Springs Series
To Charm a Scarred Cowboy
Kiss of the Texas Maverick
Vow of the Texas Cowboy
The Accidental Mail Order Bride
Starry-Eyed Mail Order Bride
An Inconvenient Mail Order Bride
Amelia's Storm

The Bluebonnet Brides Collection
Mail Order Grace
Mail Order Rescue
Mail Order Faith
Mail Order Hope
Mail Order Destiny
Love's Destiny

Sign up at www.charlottedearing.com to be notified of special offers and announcements.

Printed in Great Britain
by Amazon